AMERICAN TRASH

ANDY RAUSCH

WARNING

This novel contains a plethora of things that may be considered offensive by the easily offended. If you are one of those people, do us both a favor and skip this.

"I always felt, you don't have a good time doin' crime, you may as well find a job."

ELMORE LEONARD, *RAYLAN*

"Practically every fella that breaks the law has a danged good reason, to his own way of thinking..."

JIM THOMPSON, *POP. 1280*

This book is dedicated first to Kristin, who was with me when I wrote it, and second to Tom Leins, who showed me the beauty in grit.

ONE

THERE ARE TOO many guys packed inside Reverend Sammy's rundown trailer and it smells like a mixture of stale farts, body odor, and cigar smoke. There's new blood here today. I know the kid's fucked from the git-go. I don't know how I know, but I do. The kid, Travis, is young, probably twenty or so. Too blond and too eager; he's about as bright-eyed and bushy-tailed as a horny jackrabbit coked to the gills. All he wants is a job at the carnival, but I know Reverend Sammy's gonna make us kill the poor dumb bastard. I look over at my best friend, Cutter, and he looks back, and in that half-second exchange of glances I know we're on the same page.

Travis is sitting at the table, looking across at Sammy. The kid's eyes are wide and excited. Sammy's eyes are dark and flat like a creature of the night that's waiting to kill you and pick the meat off your bones. I know Sammy well and yet, looking at him now, *I'm* scared. I wonder if Travis is scared. Or if he even has an inkling that he *should* be scared.

Travis is chattery, telling Sammy a hundred reasons why he's always dreamt of being a carny. I think the kid is legit, just some poor dumb schmuck who wandered in off the streets looking for a job, but

I can see Sammy isn't buying it. Sammy has always been a paranoid fuck, but that's how he got to the top of the food chain; that's why he's the boss of the biggest criminal operation in the Ozarks. But now Sammy's using enough Oxy to kill an elephant, and there's no way on God's green earth this kid is getting out of here alive.

Travis is too educated. He probably only has a year or two of juco, but that's more than any of us. He's too blond. Look at him for God's sake, sitting there with his spiky hair, looking like a surfer who got lost and washed up in Missouri. There's something off about him, sure, but not in a working-for-the-feds way, but more in a he-doesn't-fucking-fit-here kind of way. But good for him. At least that's what I would say in any other circumstance; in a circumstance where he wasn't about to be killed.

Sammy is sitting there at the table, too big to properly fit in his chair. He's staring at Travis, sizing him up, but he's already made up his mind. I glance around at everyone else in the room—everyone who is not Sammy or Travis—and I can see we all know the play. Cracker Jack is sitting on the busted-up couch beside Cutter, and I'm on a raggedy-assed old recliner that's probably as old as Sammy.

Sammy's eyes narrow and he tells the kid, "These are my guys." He motions towards the couch. "That's Cracker Jack. He's the tough old sumbitch with all the tats. And that crazy spic next to him, that's Cutter."

Jesus Christ. I realize now that the meth isn't just making the old man paranoid, it's making him sloppy. If Sammy believes Travis is working for the feds, why the fuck is he telling him our names?

The kid, still smiling, looks at Cutter. "How'd you get that name?"

Cutter looks at me, grinning. Then his gaze turns towards Travis. "You're gonna find out soon enough, kid."

We all chuckle and Travis does too. He believes he's in on the joke, and his smile doesn't waver. He's grinning big like any one of the kids I see here at prize alley who've just spent ten bucks to win a prize that was made in Taiwan and cost us thirty cents. Sammy points to me. "This mean bastard behind you, that's Billy." I don't smile. Instead I'm thinking about Sammy calling me a mean bastard. I want to object, but I know he's right. And coming from Reverend Sammy, the cruelest man I've ever known, it says a lot.

"These guys are gonna take you to Branson and have you fill out the necessary forms," Sammy says around the fat cigar he's smoking.

Travis looks at him happily. "You mean I got the job?"

The old bald motherfucker reaches his meaty hand out across the table for the kid to shake. Travis shakes it, and that seals the deal.

We all stand and prepare to take him away. To search him for a wire. To beat the shit out of him. To kill him and saw his body into little bitty pieces. To bury him deep in the woods in three or four different holes. Cracker Jack, Cutter, and I all watch as Travis thanks Sammy for giving him the job he's always wanted. We're tired and we all sigh at the same time. None of us mind killing folks, but lately it's been tough. Now that Sammy is paranoid and on edge, life feels like a shitty, less-funny version of *Groundhog Day*; a tiresome loop of killing, cutting, and digging graves.

As the three of us lead Travis out to Cutter's old Caddy, Travis tells us about his little girl in Utah and about how he's working here to send her money, so she'll be okay. Again, I sigh.

Some days I wish I'd never come to work here.

TWO

YEAR ONE

NOT EVERY CARNY IS A CRIMINAL, but every carny at Funland sure the hell is. It's a hell of a place, Funland. Is it a carnival, or is it a criminal enterprise? The answer is simple: it's both.

You might be asking yourself how I came to work for such a no-good sonofabitch as Reverend Sammy in a tenth-rate carnival/crime family smack dab in the middle of the Ozarks. And you know what? Sometimes I ask myself that, too.

Aside from this possibly being a punishment for some wicked shit I did in a now-forgotten past life—a scenario I consider frequently—this is how it all went down. There's a smarmy fat-fuck lawyer named Richie Marks who lives in St. Louis. He's a duplicitous, shady motherfucker, even by lawyer standards. He specializes in defending scum. Guilty scum. So, of course, he's had plenty of dealings with Reverend Sammy and his crew. But Richie is more than just a lawyer; he doubles as a scout for Funland. So, every now and then when he comes across someone he thinks has just the right kind of criminal potential, he calls Sammy. That's what happened with me.

I wasn't privy to the conversation, but this is how I imagine it:

Richie calls Sammy. Sammy is in his trailer, smoking a fat cigar and getting head from some young runaway—that's his M.O.; he loves head, and he loves young runaways. Sammy begrudgingly answers the phone.

"Who the fuck is this?"

"Hey Sammy, it's me, Richie."

"Okay, what?"

"I got a new prospect for you."

"Oh yeah?" Sammy asks, only the slightest bit interested. I say this because nothing ever makes Sammy too interested or excited. *Nothing.* I used to think I was just misreading him, but I wasn't. That's just him—a mean, disinterested old prick.

Richie says, "I got this kid, Billy Hanson, over in lockup."

"Tell me about him," Sammy says as he watches the little skank's head bob up and down on his prick.

"Billy's the kinda kid who don't give a fuck. The cops tell him they've got him dead to rights and he's gonna do serious time, but he just looks 'em in the eyes and tells 'em to go fuck their grannies with a spiked dildo."

"Yeah? How old is this kid?"

"He's twenty-three," Richie says, "but he's smarter than twenty-three."

"What was the crime they got him for?"

Richie laughs. "*This time?* This time he stole a car that was sittin' in the parking lot of a gas station. The dumb bitch who owned it just left it sittin' there unattended. But the thing is, Billy stole it without realizin' there was a baby in the backseat."

"Oh shit."

"You bet your ass, 'oh shit'," Richie says. "But this kid Billy, he sees the baby back there, so he drops the car off in the parking lot over at Barnes Jewish. He's a criminal, but he's not tryin' to steal a baby. What he tells me, this kid, is he knew he could make a profit off sellin' the baby to some sex freak or some broad who can't have a kid of her own, but he could see the trouble there. He knew if he did that, he could go away for a long stretch, and he didn't want that. On top of that, Billy said he didn't feel right takin' somebody's kid."

"Yeah?" Sammy asks as he uses his dick to smear cum on the skank's face.

"We get to talkin', and he tells me he really loves doin' criminal shit," Richie says. "He tells me he knows he could get a straight job. Says he used to work at a porn store out on the highway and made decent money, but he says he really loves committing crime. So, I say, 'What kinda crime?' He looks me in the eye and says, 'Anything really. I'm down for whatever so long as it's against the law.' I'm tellin' you the kid gets off on criminal shit the same way the rest of us get off bustin' nuts. He's an arch fuckin' criminal, this kid."

There's a pause and then Sammy says, "So if they couldn't tie him to the car, how come he's in jail?"

Richie laughs. "A witness saw him take the car, but when they stuck him in the lineup, she wasn't sure enough to ID him. The cops know it was Billy, so they're tryin' to convince her to say it was him, but she won't do it. She's one of those goody-two-shoes liberal types, wants to be completely sure before sendin' somebody upstate."

"Right."

"So, the cops know our boy Billy stole the car, but they can't stick him with the crime. So, they run his name in their computer and find out he's got a bench warrant in Chicago for some tickets. No big deal, but for now they've got him in lockup."

"You can get him out?" Sammy asks as he stands, pulling his pants up.

"I can and I will."

"I wanna meet him. Can you arrange it?"

"Of course," Richie says. "Ask and ye shall receive."

And that's how I became a blip on Reverend Sammy's radar.

THREE

Richie drives me out to Funland, which is a four-hour drive. Funland is a stationary carnival about twenty miles outside of Branson. Funland is where Reverend Sammy and the rest of his crew work and live. When Richie drops me off, I have no idea this is gonna be my home from here on.

A forty-something woman, Barb, who looks like she might be semi-attractive in a rough, older woman way if she took a shower and cleaned up, leads me to Sammy's trailer. The beat up, dented-to-hell trailer has a green stripe down the side and looks like it was made in the 1950s. Barb says in a raspy voice, "Go on in, sugar." I start to knock, but she stops me. "You don't need to knock," she says. "Sammy knows you're comin'. Just go on in." I swing the door open and there's a big fat bald sonofabitch sitting there, smoking the biggest cigar I've ever seen and getting head from some skinny methed-out chick. He's facing me, the table in front of him, and all I can see of the girl is the back of her sandy-blonde head. Her entire body is smushed down under the table and her head is knocking against the bottom of it, over and over like a knock-knock joke with no payoff. Her skinny chicken legs are sticking out behind her and she's wearing worn-out flip-flops with holes in the soles.

The guy, muscly-fat like Harvey Keitel, looks at me, completely oblivious to the girl. "You Billy?"

I tell him I am. I don't know anything about this guy other than the fact they call him Reverend Sammy, but I know enough to be afraid. Sometimes you can just tell. It's a sense you get that that someone has seen and done some really vile shit and is capable of doing a lot more. Sammy looks like he's sixty if he's a day. He points to a chair—the same chair I'll sit in years later when Sammy has a similar interview with Travis—and tells me to sit, so I do.

"You got long hair," he says. "What are you, some kinda rock star?"

"No, sir," I say. "I just like my hair long."

"Fair enough. Richie tells me you're a criminal."

I nod. "I guess I've broken my fair share of laws."

"He tells me you *like* committing crimes. Says you get off on it. Is that true?"

"I do," I say. "It gives me a rush."

"Like a drug?"

"More," I say. "More than any drug I've ever done."

Sammy stares at me, judging me, trying to understand. "What all drugs have you done?"

"All of 'em," I say. "You name it. If it can be snorted, injected, smoked, swallowed, whatever, I've done it."

Sammy starts to say something but suddenly yelps in pain. He looks down at the girl, who has stopped. *"What's wrong?"* she screeches.

Sammy glares at her. "You fuckin' bit me, you whore."

"I'm sorry," she says fearfully. Sammy responds by punching her in the side of her head. She moans and slumps down, her head lowered to his shin, and her body slides out from under the table a bit. She's crying and moaning like an injured puppy. Sammy says, "You get back up here and finish what you started. This is like

8

when you was a kid. You don't leave until you've finished your supper."

The girl slowly maneuvers herself back into place and returns to work.

Sammy levels his gaze at me. "Do you know what I do here?"

"It's some sort of carnival," I say. I have a sense that it's more, but I don't know what, so I leave it at that.

Sammy chuckles. "That's what everybody sees, but there's more. I do a *lot* more. I do the kind of shit you like doing." He stares at me for a moment, giving me time to comprehend. "Do you understand?"

"I think so," I say. And I do, but I'm only half right. I know Sammy is a criminal, but I haven't an inkling as to how expansive his operation is.

His eyes narrow and his demeanor intensifies. "If I hired you and paid you good money to come work for me, would you do anything I ask you to do?"

I consider it. I have a good idea what he's asking. I nod. "I got nothing else going on."

Sammy's face lights up and he smiles a big, wicked smile. "What if I told you to shoot somebody?"

"And kill 'em?" I ask without skipping a beat. "Or just maim 'em?"

"Either one."

Now it's my turn to smile. "As long as the money's good, they're shot."

"What if I ask you to shoot a cop?"

My smile grows wider. "I'd do that shit for free."

Sammy chuckles. Now he makes a funny face and sits back, closing his eyes and moaning softly, and I have to watch as the old bastard has an orgasm. The girl makes a gulping sound and then pulls back and chokes for a moment. Sammy watches this gleefully. Then he looks at me. "This is my niece, Bella," he says. "Say hello to Billy, Bella." A few seconds pass and Bella manages a choked, "Hello, Billy." This makes the sadistic fucker chuckle again.

Bella's ass is facing me and Sammy palms it. "I'd like you to have a piece of this before you go," he says. "She's got a nice tight butthole, this one." Sammy slides his finger down, burying it knuckle deep in her ass. Then he raises his finger and sucks it clean as he grins at me.

This is my introduction to Reverend Sammy and all the crazy criminal shit that goes on at Funland.

FOUR

WHEN EVENING COMES, Funland is lit up brighter than Einstein with a hundred-watt light bulb rammed up his ass. The amusement park is a different place after dark. It's magical. There's music and flashing lights and carnival barking. Best of all, the place is jam-packed with suckers, all more than happy to fork over their hard-earned dough.

Sammy has just introduced me to Cracker Jack, who will become my mentor, as well as a father figure. "Stick close to him," Sammy said. "Cracker Jack's been around the block a time or ten. You'll learn a lot from him." So here I am now, following Cracker Jack as he gives me the grand tour of the park. I know right off the bat that he's a tough sonofabitch. He's bald like Sammy, but in a lean, muscular, beat-the-fuck-out-of-you sort of way. He's younger than Sammy by a couple of decades, but he's older than me. The guy is covered in tats ranging from primitive jail house markings—he's done stretches in Texas and Iowa—to nice custom work depicting naked women with big tits and hairy bushes, as well as Jesus Christ on the cross.

I ask him what his job is, and he laughs. "On the books, my job is general manager," he says. "That means I keep the place straight. I make sure there's no bullshit going on and no one giving the carnys a hard time." He looks at me as we walk. "But I do a lot more than that. There's a lot to my job. I'm the guy who makes sure the right palms get greased so we can operate here without any trouble. Basically, it's my job to make sure everybody's happy."

"What if somebody's unhappy?" I ask.

Cracker Jack tilts his head and gives me a mischievous sideways grin. "Then I gotta bust somebody's head open." I don't know it yet, but Cracker Jack can fight like a madman. He'll tell me later that he learned how to fight behind bars, and he'll say it was the one thing that kept him sane during that time. But to be honest, "sane" is not a word I'd use to describe Cracker Jack.

We're walking down the fairway, and I'm gawking in amazement like a tourist fresh off the bus. I've never been to a carnival. I grew up with my uncle who was too poor to take me to anything like this, and later with my grandparents who were too old. Cracker Jack points towards the game booths and tells me Sammy had considered having me work one. Cracker Jack says that's where he started when he first came to Funland. But he says Sammy has a different job in mind for me now and that I'll have to wait to find out what it is.

As we walk, a girl with a great set of tits and a pair of shorts that are practically painted on her ass walks past us. My eyes are following her ass, and Cracker Jack sees me. "Watch yourself," he says. "Those young girls'll get your tit in a ringer." I tell him I think she's nineteen or twenty. He laughs. "They're all nineteen or twenty until you get into the courtroom." He says this in a manner that suggests he's had some experience with this, but I don't ask.

When we reach the dunk tank, Cracker Jack stops to watch. We're about twenty feet away. There's some poor bastard dressed like a clown sitting up there on a perch in the tank, egging customers on. He's telling a fat guy that he's fat, which of course makes the guy angry. And that's the point.

"Look at this fat fuck," Cracker Jack says. "He's pissed off because Ray called him fat and told him his clothes look like they're five sizes too small. You get a guy good and steamed like that, he'll spend every dollar he's got on balls to throw and try to knock you off that stoop. That's the beauty of it." He looks at me. "You see Ray sitting up there? Listen to him. Pissing people off is an art, and he's got it mastered. He's the best I've ever seen."

We watch as the fat man hurls ball after ball, missing one after the other. Finally, the guy gets steamed and storms off into the crowd. Ray yells at him from the dunk tank and tells him he's a fat crybaby loser. To this, the fat crybaby loser spins around and flips him the bird. And that's the end of the fat guy. Within a minute, another guy steps up and pays money to be made fun of and try to dunk Ray.

"He's good," I say. "I'll bet he brings in good money."

Cracker Jack nods. "Yeah, he does."

"What happens when Ray pisses somebody off and they attack him?"

Cracker Jack smiles, tapping his chest. "That's where I come in. If they do, I promise you they'll wish they hadn't." I laugh and he looks at me, serious as a heart attack. "You think you can do what he's doing?"

"What?" I ask. "Piss people off?"

"Yeah."

I laugh. "My baby's mama said I pissed her off all the time. Said nobody had ever pissed her off more."

Cracker Jack doesn't smile. "I'm serious, Billy. You think you can do this?"

I tell him I can.

"Good," he says. "We're gonna try you out tomorrow."

I'm startled by this. "I'm gonna be up there making fun of people, trying to make them knock me into the water?"

"You got a problem with that?"

"No, not at all. But what if I'm not good enough?"

He puts his hand on my shoulder. "You'll be fine. We'll work with you if you need work, but I think you're gonna be great."

"What makes you say that?"

He grins big. "I know an asshole when I see one."

We both chuckle.

"What about Ray?" I ask. "Is he quitting?"

"He is. He just don't know yet, so keep this under your hat."

"I don't have a hat."

Cracker Jack levels his gaze at me. "Just keep your fuckin' mouth shut, okay?"

"Sure," I say. "But what happened with Ray?"

Cracker Jack looks at me in a way that suggests he wants to smile, but he doesn't. "You know how I said he had a talent for pissing people off? Well, he pissed off the wrong person. He pissed off Reverend Sammy, and kid, let me tell you, you don't wanna piss off Reverend Sammy."

FIVE

When the night is over and the lights go down, we watch Ray climb down from the tank. "I can't wait to change my clothes," he tells his assistant. "I'm as cold as a lesbian librarian in an igloo." Cracker Jack and I stand there, leaning against a snack bar shack that's been closed all night.

Cracker Jack looks at me. "You smoke?"

"I do," I say, fishing the pack out of my jeans pocket.

"Can I bum one?"

"Sure."

I hand him the cigarette. He holds it up and looks at it like he's examining a dog turd. "What kind is this?"

"Marlboro menthols."

As he raises it to his lips, he says, "I don't like menthols. I don't like Marlboros either. Get Camels next time."

I stare at him as he lights up, trying to decide whether or not he's joking. I conclude he's not. I look away, but I'm still thinking about the amount of gall it takes for someone to demand such a thing. But Funland is a new world filled with new rules that I've got to learn quickly.

We both smoke about half our cigarettes and then Cracker Jack drops his and crushes it beneath his boot. "Let's go."

"Where we going?"

"Shut up and come on."

He leads me back behind the tents and buildings to an area where there are twenty or thirty trailers set up. "This is where we live," he says, continuing to walk. I'm right behind him and I ask where I'll be staying. He says, "You're gonna stay with Linda for a while." I ask him who Linda is. He tells me she's part of the freak show and that she's billed as "Linda the Dog-Face Girl." I follow him, wondering what the hell a dog-face girl looks like.

Cracker Jack makes his way to a decrepit trailer and bangs on the door. A moment later the door opens, and Ray is standing there wearing boxer shorts and an open robe. He still has the clown makeup on. He makes a confused face. "What's going on?"

"We're goin' for a ride," Cracker Jack says, as cool as a Fall breeze.

Ray's expression changes to one of concern. "Okay, then just let me put on my clothes."

"No, you'll go as you are."

Ray looks down at his bare stomach. "But I ain't got no clothes on!"

Cracker Jack steps towards him and growls, "Not another fuckin' word, Ray."

Ray looks at me. "Who the fuck are you, kid?"

Cracker Jack steps forward and punches Ray hard in the nuts. Ray howls and doubles over, holding himself. "Don't disrespect the kid," Cracker Jack says. "Now tell him you're sorry." Ray is still doubled over, but he says, "I'm sorry." Soon we're all three walking between the trailers. We move in file with Cracker Jack leading the way. Ray is in the middle and I'm in the rear.

"What's this all about?" Ray asks nervously.

Cracker Jack stops and looks back at Ray with fire in his eyes. He points at him and says, "You shut your fuck flap is what this is about." Then Cracker Jack turns and resumes walking.

A moment later he arrives at another trailer. He bangs on the door.

"Alright, alright," comes an annoyed voice.

The door opens and a tough-looking little Mexican who's about my age pops out. He looks at Cracker Jack, then at Ray, then at me. "What the fuck is all this? You guys havin' a party, and nobody told me?"

"I'm inviting you now," Cracker Jack says. "Sammy wants us to have a talk with Ray."

Ray gasps. The little Mexican looks at me. "And who the fuck is this?"

Cracker Jack turns towards me, smiling. "This is the new kid. His name is Billy."

The Mexican gives me a strange look. "*Billy?* Fuck kinda name is that?"

Cracker Jack chuckles. "You'll like him. He's an asshole like you."

The Mexican is dressed in jeans and an Anthrax shirt. He steps out and closes the door. Then he walks towards me with a big smile on his face and holds his hand out for me to shake. "Hiya, Billy, ya fucker. I'm Cutter."

I say hello and shake his hand. Then the four of us make our way back through the darkened carnival. As we walk, nobody says a word. We walk out through the front entrance and go to Cutter's 1980-something baby-blue Caddy. We all get in and Cutter gets behind the wheel. Ray is next to him in the passenger seat. Cracker Jack and I are in back.

Ray turns so we can all see him. "Did I do something wrong?"

"Fuck you," Cracker Jack growls. "You know what you did."

Ray looks genuinely confused. "I don't. I don't have a clue."

Cutter turns and looks back. "What did this prick do? I don't know either."

"He fucked Sammy's niece, Bella."

Cutter starts giggling. "Well, who hasn't?"

"Ain't that the truth," Cracker Jack says, chuckling. "But we did it because Sammy told us to. It was different with Ray."

Ray looks at us with an expression of terror. "I didn't know."

"Bella is the boss' favorite niece," says Cracker Jack. "Her pussy is invitation-only."

"Her asshole, too," Cutter says, chuckling.

Ray is sobbing now. "I didn't know. I swear I didn't." Then he looks back at Cracker Jack. "I thought she was old enough. She said she was twenty-three."

"She is," Cutter says. "But that ain't the point."

Ray starts begging for forgiveness, but no one acknowledges his pleas. As he's begging, Cracker Jack asks Cutter, "Did you bring the bone saw?"

SIX

WE'RE in some woods off Highway 86 that a friend of Reverend Sammy's owns. Sammy hides his problems six feet deep underground out here. We've been in these dark woods for a few hours and Ray is digging his own grave. Cracker Jack, Cutter, and me are all standing around watching the prick dig. It's hot and humid, and the mosquitoes want my blood. It's always been that way for me. When I was a kid, my grandma used to say it had something to do with the amount of iron in my blood, but I don't know. Grandma had dementia and she used to say a lot of stupid shit.

Despite the heat, the sweat, the darkness, and the mosquitoes, none of this would be quite as bad if Ray wasn't complaining the whole time. I get why he's complaining—I mean, he's about to die— but that doesn't make it any less annoying.

He stops digging and he's standing there knee-deep in the hole looking at us, his face half-illuminated by the lantern Cracker Jack is holding. Ray says, "You know, we could just skip all this."

"Oh yeah?" Cutter says, playing along.

"Yeah," Ray says, real serious. "You could just let me go and I could move away someplace far away."

"Yeah?" Cutter asks. "Where would you go?"

"Canada maybe. I always did like hockey."

"Where would that leave us?" Cracker Jack asks. "I mean, why would we let you go? What's in it for us?"

Ray looks down, searching for the answer. "I don't have any money if that's what you mean. But it would be a nice thing to do, you know? Good karma. I never done nothing to anybody. I'm a good guy." He looks at Cutter. "You know me, Cutter. How long you and me been friends?"

"About five years," Cutter says.

"Right," Ray says, nodding. "Five years. You know I don't deserve this."

Cutter stares at him. "You wanna know what I know, Ray?"

Ray stares at him, and nobody says a word. Finally, Cutter says, "I know you better get to digging and shut your fucking dick-hole. If you don't, this is liable to go a whole lot worse for you."

Ray stands there looking at him, and his desperation hangs in the air as thick as the humidity. "You're already gonna kill me," Ray says. "What's worse than that?"

Cracker Jack chuckles.

Cutter says, "You keep fuckin' around, you're gonna find out."

Ray resumes digging. He digs for a while and the rest of us talk. Cracker Jack explains to me that Reverend Sammy is called reverend because he's an actual minister, which blows my mind. He tells me Sammy's got a church in Branson.

"How does that work?" I ask. "How can he be a minister and still do..." I think about the words and then look at Ray and say, "all *this*?"

Cutter and Cracker Jack chuckle. I think Ray might have chuckled if he wasn't bawling like a damn baby.

"He says he doesn't curse too much or drink all that much alcohol," Cutter says.

"And he don't kill nobody on the sabbath," Cracker Jack adds.

Time passes and we watch Ray dig a little more. After a while, Cutter says, "I'll tell you what, Ray. I'll give you a chance to run. If you make it, we'll let you run off to Canada." He turns to Cracker Jack. "What do you think? Does that sound fair to you?"

"That's fair," Cracker Jack says. "And it's dark out here. You might make it."

"Get up outta that hole," Cutter demands.

Ray struggles to get out, but he manages.

"Get ready to run, you fuck," Cracker Jack says.

"You ready, Ray?" Cutter asks.

Ray looks nervous as hell but says he's ready. He squares himself to run.

"Maybe I should do some stretching first," he suggests.

Cracker Jack chuckles again. "This fuckin' guy."

"Don't push your luck," Cutter says. "We're gonna give you a full minute before we start blasting, so you better run like a Kenyan on fire."

"On your mark," Cracker Jack says. "Get ready..."

Ray is about to break into a sprint when Cutter shoots him in the leg with his .45. The muzzle flash lights up the dark woods and Ray howls with pain, falling back into the hole he's just dug. Cutter raises the .45 towards Ray again, but Cracker Jack stops him. "Give the gun to Billy."

I've got nothing against killing somebody, but I've never done it before. I always figured the day would come, but I didn't think it would be like this. I don't know if I'm ready. I look at Cracker Jack and Cutter, searching for help, but I find none.

"Go ahead, kid," Cracker Jack says.

This is a test and I have to pass it. I don't wanna end up dead in these woods next to Ray and whoever the fuck else is out here. I'm standing over the hole looking down at Ray. I raise the pistol, aiming it at his face. He looks up at me, crying. "You don't gotta do this, kid."

But he's wrong. I do.

I squeeze the trigger and Ray finally shuts the fuck up.

SEVEN

On Sunday nights the Funland employees congregate at the Bowl-Mor, which is a bowling alley Reverend Sammy owns. Sammy owns all kinds of businesses from strip clubs to car lots to you fucking name it. All the Funland folks hang out at the Bowl-Mor, but the parties aren't just for us. You go, you're likely to see just about anyone who's somebody in Missouri. Cutter says he saw that rapper who wears the Band-Aid on his cheek there once, but I'm not sure if he's telling the truth.

This is my first Bowl-Mor party. I'm still tired since we were up all goddamn night killing and burying Ray, but I snorted some crushed Adderall before we came. I still feel tired as fuck, at least mentally, but my body feels like it might launch into outer space like a rocket at any moment. God, I love Adderall. I'm un-medicated bipolar, so my love of speed is probably just me searching for the high of being manic.

Cracker Jack, Cutter, and me are all standing in the middle of the pool room, ready to mingle. No one is talking to us, and we're not talking to anyone either. But we *look* like we're fucking mingling. I'm wearing a black Judas Priest shirt, Cracker Jack is wearing a

Hawaiian shirt with baggy jeans that look like they're out of a '90s rap video, and Cutter is still wearing the same Anthrax shirt he had on last night.

"What the fuck is this?" Cracker Jack asks, grabbing the front of Cutter's shirt.

"What do you mean?" Cutter asks, visibly offended.

"You're wearing the same shit you had on last night."

"So what?" Cutter asks, clearly annoyed. "It didn't get dirty. And my armpits didn't smell it up. Besides, what are you, the fucking clothes police?"

"Jesus, man. You need to take a shower. You smell like a dirty-assed bum who just had a train run on him by all the other dirty bums."

I chuckle. Cutter is annoyed with Cracker Jack, but he doesn't want to tussle with him, so he turns on me. *What the fuck, Billy?*

I'm just standing here holding my beer. "What?"

Cutter is full-on coming at me now. *Why the fuck did you laugh?*

I take a drink of my beer, trying to look like I'm not scared of these crazy motherfuckers. "I didn't mean anything," I say. "I was just laughing at what Cracker Jack said."

Cutter points his finger in my face. "You better watch that shit, Billy"

I pretend not to give a shit.

"Look at this fuckin' guy," Cracker Jack says. We both look where he's looking and see a stuffy-looking prick with a younger blonde on his arm. The guy looks completely out of place here.

"Who's that?" I ask.

Cracker Jack and Cutter chuckle.

"That prick is the mayor of Branson," Cutter says. "Can you believe that? This fuckin' guy's out rubbing elbows with lowlife criminals, not even trying to hide it."

"And the girl with him?" Cracker Jack says. "The guy's married, and that's not his wife."

"Maybe we should blackmail him," I suggest, thinking I've found an angle. "All we gotta do is go over and threaten to call his wife unless he gives us a thousand bucks."

"A thousand bucks?" Cracker Jack says. "You need to raise your sights a little."

Cutter leans in. "Anybody you see here; you don't fuck with them. This is Sammy's place, and these are his people. Some of them, like that rat fuck there, are just here because Sammy needs something from them. But either way, they're his people."

"His people?" I ask.

Cracker Jack looks at me solemnly. "You see 'em here, you don't fuck with 'em. Simple as that."

I nod in understanding.

"Besides," Cracker Jack says, "Sammy has a strict nothing-on-the-side rule. He doesn't want anybody doing side hustles because that shit could come back on him. You get caught; it brings him undesired attention. Besides, he gets a piece of everything you make, so you gotta include him if you're doing any slick shit."

The conversation soon shifts to football and other unimportant random shit. We mingle a little and I talk to some women, but there's no one here I'm all that interested in. Well, there's one—a little redhead named Grace who works the counter—but she says she's got a boyfriend. Even worse, her boyfriend is a cop. A fucking cop if you can believe that. I tell her I'm not giving up, so she should expect to see more of me. She just laughs.

Cracker Jack, Cutter, and me stay another hour before we decide it's time to go. Cracker Jack is on his Harley, and I rode with Cutter. Both vehicles are parked next to each other out on the edge of the dark parking lot. As we're walking out, Cutter is telling a story I suspect to be bullshit about him having sex with a girl, her sister, and their mom at the same time. As we're walking, I hear Cracker Jack say, *"Hey you! What the fuck?!"* I look up and see that there's a homeless man standing beside Cracker Jack's Harley. He looks at us with a frightened expression and takes a step back. "I wasn't doin' nothing," he says.

"You better not be," Cutter says.

Cracker Jack walks over to inspect the motorcycle but finds nothing out of the ordinary. "You shouldn't mess with a man's motorcycle. There's a lot of things you can mess with, but you never mess with a man's woman, his kids, or his motorcycle."

"I'm sorry," the homeless man says. He pauses for a moment and says, "I hate to bother you gentlemen, but could any of you spare ten bucks?"

Cutter leans back and his eyes are big. "*Whoa!* The nerve of this fuck!" He turns towards the homeless man. "You don't fuck around, do you? I mean, you don't just ask for spare change, or even a dollar. No, you go full tilt and ask for the whole tenner!"

Cracker Jack and I laugh. This embarrasses the homeless man, and he looks at Cutter and mutters, "Fuck you!" Cracker Jack and I laugh harder, pissing Cutter off.

Cracker Jack is egging Cutter on, trying to make him angrier. "You hear that? He said fuck you!" Cracker Jack laughs and then adds, "The way you smell, he probably thinks you're a homeless bum, too!" Cracker Jack and I are laughing hard now. The homeless man looks at us, confused. Cutter steps towards him and I cringe, thinking Cutter is about to knock him out. But he doesn't. Instead Cutter pulls out a butterfly knife and buries the blade in the man's neck. Blood spurts out like a geyser, and the man makes a gurgling sound, slowly sliding down to the pavement. Cutter pulls the blade from his throat.

"*What the fuck did you do that for?!*" Cracker Jack says.

Cutter looks at us. He's got blood all over his face and his shirt is covered in bum's blood. "Fuck this guy," he says. "I'm not gonna let some goddamn hobo disrespect me!"

Cracker Jack and I both turn to look at the Bowl-Mor to see if anyone has witnessed all this. No one has. At least not yet.

"We gotta get this fucker in the trunk and take him out to the woods," Cutter says.

"Damn," I say. I don't mean to say it, it just comes out. But thankfully, no one cares.

Cutter looks apologetic now. "Look, I'm sorry, but this fuck—"

Cracker Jack interrupts and says, "Just open the goddamn trunk." He looks at me. "Grab the guy's legs, Billy." This irritates me, but I do it. I've been working at Funland for about twenty-four hours and I've already had to deal with two dead bodies. The trunk is open now and Cracker Jack and I carry the body over. Cracker Jack glares at Cutter and says, "This should be you carrying this fuckin' body, Cutter. This is what you do."

"What?" Cutter asks. "What do I do?"

We're lowering the bum into the trunk when Cracker Jack snaps, "You always do this! Always!"

"What do I do?"

"You fuck things up," Cracker Jack says angrily as he rubs his bloody hands together.

"That's fucked up," Cutter says as he shuts the trunk.

I get in the car and we head back to the woods.

EIGHT

A couple times a week Cutter and I visit the Booby Trap, which is a strip club Sammy owns in Branson. It's our job to go and look the place over to make sure everything's running as it should. If Cal, the manager, has any problems or concerns, we swoop in and take care of them. We do it ourselves if we can, and if not, we take it to back to Sammy. We act as go-betweens since Sammy never sets foot in the place. The fucking guy owns a strip club but believes it's sinful to go inside. Which is fine because I've got a side hustle selling pills and H there and I know if Sammy finds out, I'm gonna be in a world of shit. Cutter knows I sell out of the club, but he doesn't care. We've become tight in the six months since I started at Funland.

We're in the club and Cutter's back in the VIP room getting special treatment from Kammie, this blonde stripper he likes. Cutter and I have an unspoken rule that he doesn't say anything about me selling drugs, and I don't say anything about him routinely seeing a stripper who sells pussy to truckers. He's back there doing God knows what to Kammie, and I'm sitting at a table watching this black girl, Dominique, doing all kinds of freaky shit on stage. I like black chicks, but I still haven't fucked Dominique. As I watch her grinding now, I'm thinking that needs to be rectified soon. Lately I've just been banging Linda the dog-faced bitch, which isn't so bad really. Linda's face looks like Chewbacca, but her body is actually quite lovely.

There's a smattering of guys in the club, which is dark save for the flashing blue strobe lights. The music is throbbing—some hippity-hoppity shit I'm not familiar with—and there's a dude in a ball cap sitting near the front who keeps looking back at me. He's done this five or six times now and it's clear he either wants to buy drugs or fuck me. I'm hoping it's drugs because I don't want to have to stomp him flat. It's not that I've got anything against homos—hell, I let my cousin Jarrod suck me off for meth a couple times—but I've got to maintain my rep, and that shit doesn't fly at Funland.

Finally, after a few songs have played, ball cap dude gets up and walks back to my table. He looks at me and smirks, nodding at an empty chair. "Can I sit?"

I ask, "Who the fuck are you?" He puts out his hand for me to shake—I don't shake it—and he says, "We've got a mutual friend." I ask him who and he says, "Terry. He buys offa you every week." I ponder this for a minute and come up with a face. "Terry?" I ask. "Fat fuck with bad complexion, wears a cowboy hat?" He says yep, that's him, so I tell ball cap dude we have to go outside.

We go to the parking lot and ball cap dude is looking around nervously, and I conclude he doesn't do this very often. I tell him the price and he hands me a sweaty wad of bills. He gives me $10 too much, but I pocket it anyway. Because fuck this guy. I hand him the baggie, he examines it, and then he smiles this weird goofy smile. I don't understand the meaning of the smile until he reaches into his pocket and produces a wallet with a badge.

"You have the right to remain silent..."

Fuck my life.

NINE

I've been in the holding cell for about two hours when a deputy strides in, opens the cage, and says, "You get to go home." I ask him what the deal is, and he apologizes. "We're sorry to have bothered you, Mr. Hanson. We didn't know who you were." I'm not entirely sure what this means, but I assume it's because I work for Reverend Sammy. The deputy releases me with zero paperwork and walks me to the front door.

I open the door and step out into the bright sun. Sammy and Cracker Jack are standing there waiting for me. They both have serious expressions and I wonder if Sammy is going to have me clipped. He steps towards me and puts his big hairy ape-man arm around me. He pulls me close and I'm fucking scared.

He looks me in my eyes. "Don't ever do this shit again. You're one of my guys, so I'm gonna let it slide this once."

I exhale, not even realizing I've been holding my breath. "I was afraid you were gonna be pissed."

The look in his eyes freezes my blood. "Don't get it twisted, kid, I *am* pissed. I'm super fuckin' pissed because I trusted you and you fucked up. You took a dump on my trust." He pauses and stares at me, and the look he gives me is even scarier than the previous one. "I'm giving you this one get out of jail free card. One. Just one. Don't ever do this again, you got it?"

I tell him I do. He leans in and whispers with hot wing breath, "You ever do anything like this again, you're gonna end up chopped up in itty bitty pieces out there in the woods with the other dumb hillbillies."

TEN

YEAR TWO

It's a hotter-than-fuck Sunday afternoon in July and we're unloading a police truck filled with guns and placing them inside a storage container. The two cops, Marshall and Grissom, are on the take. But then most of the Branson police department supplements their incomes with look-the-other-way cash from Sammy. One of the ways the cops help us is by handing over weapons they confiscate from other criminals. Missouri has more hate groups than any other state in the country, so there are always guns coming in.

It's Cracker Jack, Cutter, Artie Bisher, Cunny Jaymes, and me, along with the two cops. Cracker Jack is smoking a cigarette, supervising. Cutter and I are smoking cigarettes and assisting him in supervising, leaving all the actual work to Artie and Cunny. They're both sweating like altar boys taking loads from priests, and Artie looks like he's thirty seconds from a heat stroke, but neither of them says a word. They just keep working. Artie and Cunny are good guys, but they're way down on the totem pole, so they keep their mouths shut. If they mouth off or complain too much, they're liable to end up buried in the woods.

The cops are standing beside us, watching Artie and Cunny.

Cutter is telling us about how he believes Puerto Ricans are the best baseball players. He keeps talking about Roberto Clemente, claiming he was the best baseball player in history. I don't know anything about Roberto Clemente, and I don't care to.

Cutter looks at me. "The fuckin' guy hit over .300 in his career and had over three thousand hits. I'll bet you didn't know he played in fifteen All-Star Games." I grin and say, "I'll bet you didn't know I don't give a fuck." The cops and Cracker Jack chuckle, and Cutter's getting himself worked up. He starts to pop some shit, but the black cop, Marshall, cuts him off. "You know why Latins are so good at sports?" he asks. "Those beaners get in shape while they're swimming to America!" We all laugh, but Cutter doesn't. He just stands there glaring at Marshall.

Marshall says Cutter doesn't think the joke is funny because he's a wetback. Cutter looks him in the eyes and warns, "Say that shit again and I'll bust your fuckin' head wide open." Marshall considers responding but thinks the better of it. This is good because Marshall might be a cop, but he's also an employee of Reverend Sammy, and Sammy wouldn't think twice to have him clipped. It doesn't help that Marshall is black because Sammy doesn't care for anybody with dark skin. He doesn't care for Mexicans at all, which makes his affinity for Cutter seem strange.

We all go back to watching Artie and Cunny transferring the guns. The other cop, Grissom, looks at Cracker Jack. "You're Reverend Sammy's right-hand man?" Cracker Jack chuckles and says, "*Right-hand man?* I'm more than that." To this, Cutter asks, "What's more than a right-hand man?" I suggest maybe a dick-man is something more than a right-hand man. Cracker Jack chuckles. "There's probably a lot of people who believe I'm a dick. I've got a couple of ex-wives who definitely think so." We all laugh, and Grissom says, "Can we talk for a minute?"

Cracker Jack says, "We're talking now."

Grissom looks at us and then over at Artie and Cunny. "I meant someplace private. Someplace with less ears."

Cracker Jack motions towards us. "These are my guys. They're like the right-hand men of the right-hand man."

"Dick-men to the dick-man," I add.

"Anything you wanna say to me you can say in front of them," Cracker Jack says.

Grissom points at Artie and Cunny. "What about them?"

Cracker Jack nods towards the side of the truck. "Let's go for a walk."

Cracker Jack leads Cutter, Grissom, and me around the truck where no one can eavesdrop. Marshall stays behind to watch Artie and Cunny.

"Here I am," Cracker Jack says. "What do you need?"

Grissom looks around nervously like he expects paparazzi to spring from the bushes and snap his picture, but it's just us. He leans in and says, "My sister is fucking Bill White. Does that name ring a bell?"

Cracker Jack looks at me and Cutter. "You guys know Bill White?"

We both shrug. Cracker Jack turns back towards the cop. "Who's Bill White?"

Grissom flashes a smile. "Bill White is a rich white-collar fuck who's running for Governor. He lives in a big mansion over in Jeff City."

"Okay," Cracker Jack says.

"My sister is his mistress. White is married, has kids and a dog and all that, but he's fucking my sister."

"You must be so proud," Cutter says.

Grissom ignores this. "Here's the deal. The guy's got a great big safe filled with cash for his campaign. He keeps all his on-the-books money in a bank. But this money, it's secret. He keeps it locked in a safe inside his office."

"Where'd it come from?" Cracker Jack asks.

"How the fuck do I know?"

"How much money we talkin'?"

"My sister Kendra," Grissom says, "she saw the money. She said the rich prick showed her the money to impress her. She didn't know how much was in there, but she said it was a *lot*. She said it was more money than she'd ever seen in her life." Grissom turns and looks at me. *"Millions."*

"Okay, so what?" Cracker Jack says. "I don't know shit about safe cracking. Do you?"

"The safe has a key-code combination," Grissom says. "Kendra saw him type it into the keypad."

We all perk up.

Cracker Jack says, "She saw the combination, huh?"

Grissom is grinning like a goon. "She did. So, we're thinking, you send some of your guys in there—sometime when Bill White is off with Kendra someplace, so he won't suspect her—and they clean out the safe. Then we all get together and split it up. You guys, Reverend Sammy, Kendra, and me."

Cracker Jack nods happily. He always looks happy when he's doing gangster shit. He's like me—he does it for the love of the game. "Let me talk to Sammy about this and I'll be in touch," he says. He reaches out and pumps Grissom's hand like they're old buddies.

ELEVEN

THAT NIGHT we're back at the Bowl-Mor. The place is crowded and everyone's having a good time. There aren't any famous people tonight—no rappers or politicians—but just about everyone who works at Funland is here, drinking and having a good time.

I'm with Cutter and Cracker Jack, as always, and we've got a table. We're sharing an order of onion rings while we wait to talk to Sammy about Grissom's proposition. Cracker Jack is certain Sammy will be interested. Right now, Sammy is busy in his office, banging a teenage skank with blue hair he picked up at Mickey D's. Cutter is talking—*he's always talking*—about a chick he picked up last week at the grocery store. According to him, he fucked her inside her little Ford Fiesta in the parking lot. I look across the room at Grace, the redhead who works the counter. She's the most beautiful woman I've ever seen. I like watching her, but she hasn't even noticed I'm here.

"Sorry, guys," I say as I stand. "I'll be back."

Cutter pauses for a moment, flashes me a nasty look, and then continues with his story. But it's okay; I won't miss anything since he's already told me this story twice. I stroll across the bowling alley to the front counter. Grace looks up and sees me. She smiles, and I hope it's because she's happy to see me and not just a be-polite-to-the-fucking-customers smile.

"There you are," she says. "I haven't seen you lately."

"Have you missed me?"

"I don't know that I'd say all that."

"It's okay," I say. "We both know you want me." Of course, this is a joke. I don't know anything of the sort. I *want* her to want me, but that's the extent of it.

Her grin widens and her pretty, sparkling green eyes look at me in a way that makes my heart and my dick feel funny. "You wish," she says. And she's right—I do. I ask, "How's your boyfriend—the *cop*?" I say the word 'cop' the way other people say brain cancer or dead babies.

She stares at me, still smiling. "He's good." She pauses. "What? You don't like cops?"

"Enough about pigs. Let's talk about you and me."

Her left eyebrow raises. "There's a me and you?"

"One of these days."

"You ask me out every single week, and every week I say no."

"Not true," I say. "I didn't ask you out last week."

"Only because you weren't here."

"Okay, okay, I'll make you a deal," I say. "If you want me to quit asking you out, all you gotta do is say yes and go."

She grins a sexy grin and she bites her bottom lip. "I'll think about it."

"What does that mean?"

"The magic eight ball says try again later."

This response is unexpected and gives me hope. I'm about to say something dirty and probably fuck it all up when I feel the tap on my shoulder. I turn and see Cracker Jack. He points towards Sammy's office. "He's ready for us." I turn back to Grace and smile. "I gotta go. Duty calls."

"No rest for the wicked," she says. I'm walking backwards, still looking at her. "You think I'm wicked?"

She laughs. "No, I *know* you're wicked."

TWELVE

I WALK into Sammy's office behind Cracker Jack and Cutter. The place smells like cigar smoke and sex. I look around for the blue-haired girl, but she's already gone. I level my gaze at Sammy. "You want me to shut the door?"

He grins. "Unless you want every dumb fuck in the building to hear what we're saying, then yes, close it."

I shut the door and we all sit down in chairs facing Sammy.

Sammy looks at Cracker Jack. "So, what's the story?"

"I got a lead on a job that could make us all a lot of money."

"Oh yeah?" Sammy says. "How much we talkin'?"

"I don't know for sure, but it sounds like a fuckload."

Sammy smiles big. "How much is a fuckload?"

We all chuckle.

"I don't know, but it's a lot," Cracker Jack says. "Certainly more than I've got." He tells Sammy about Grissom, Grissom's sister, Bill White, and the safe.

"It sounds good," Sammy says, considering it. "Maybe too good."

"I think it's legit," Cracker Jack says. "This fucker Grissom, he just wants the money to fund his coke habit."

"He does coke?"

"This fucker does more coke than the four of us combined."

Sammy leans back in his chair—so far that I think he's gonna topple over. He grins big. "That's a lot of fuckin' coke!"

"You bet your ass it is," Cutter agrees.

Sammy sits there, looking down, and thinking. Then he looks at Cracker Jack. "You tell this pig I wanna sit down and talk to him about the particulars."

Cracker Jack smiles. "I'll call him tonight."

"Sounds good," Sammy says as he lights up another cigar.

"How many of those do you figure you smoke in a day?" I ask.

Sammy looks at me with a big shit-eating grin and says, "Probably less than your mom smokes cocks."

"My mom's dead," I inform him.

Sammy points a meaty finger at me and says, "In hell, Billy. She sucks cocks in hell."

I nod. He's probably right.

THIRTEEN

CUTTER and I are in the woods getting rid of this guy Jake who owed
Sammy money. Once it became clear that Jake was never gonna pay,
Sammy asked us to cancel his account. Jake owned a hardware store
off the highway, so we went to visit him as he was closing up for the
night. We had planned to take Jake out into the country somewhere
and shoot him, but things got heated and I ended up putting the claw
end of a hammer through his skull.

It was the first time I ever used a claw hammer as a weapon, and
it turned out to be way messier than I'd have imagined. Maybe it
would have been a different story if I'd used the hammer end, but it
didn't work out that way. As a result, we had to clean up brains and
blood. It was a hell of a mess. Thankfully, the floors in Jake's store
were linoleum, so the cleanup was fairly easy. We had discussed
cutting up the body inside the store, but we decided against it
because it would have increased the chances of leaving DNA behind
for nosy-ass cops to find. It would have also increased the chances of
somebody walking in and finding us there.

Cutter doesn't like it when I kill people. He likes doing it himself,
which is fine by me because I don't much care for it. Not that Cutter

and I really get to kill all that many people anyway. That's Cracker Jack's job and he's really good at it. As he likes to remind us, he was killing people when we were still kids.

Cutter is digging. I'm a couple feet away, hunkered down over Jake's stripped-down body, sawing him into little pieces. Cutter takes a break and looks at me. He starts chuckling. "You look good cutting up corpses."

"I look good?" I ask. "What? Are you hitting on me?"

"No, I'm just saying it fits you. You look like you was born to cut up bodies."

"What the fuck does that even mean?"

"From now on you're Bonesaw Billy. That's your new name! *Bonesaw Billy!*"

I roll my eyes and mutter "whatever" as I go back to sawing this dead fucker's hand off.

Cutter digs for a while, whistling as he does. I hate it when he whistles, but I don't say anything. I just keep on sawing through flesh and bone. After a while, Cutter takes another break. He loves killing guys but isn't quite as keen on burying them.

"Can I tell you something?" he asks.

"Of course," I say as I saw through Jake's thigh.

"If I tell you this, you gotta promise not to tell anybody."

"Okay, sure."

"No, I'm serious."

I stop and look at him. "Cutter, come on! I never tell nobody nothing *ever*. I don't do that. I ain't no loose-lipped Sally."

"Sure. You're right, you ain't no Sally."

I stare at him for another moment wondering what this deep dark secret I'm about to hear is.

"Okay," he says, building towards it. "You know that girl Kammie?"

"The stripper you're in love with?"

He stands there staring at me and I realize I've beaten him to the punch. "Fuck you, Billy."

"It's no big deal, man."

"How did you know? I mean... What makes you think I'm in love with her?"

I stare at him, grinning. "Bitch please. It's obvious to anyone who knows you."

He stares at me, thinking. "You think Cracker Jack knows?"

"Only if he's got two eyes and a brain." I laugh, which loosens Cutter up and he cracks a sort of half-smile.

"Okay," he says, "maybe I've got some feelings for her."

"*Some* feelings?"

He looks at me with a shy, vulnerable expression that looks strange on him.

"Okay, maybe more," he says. "But I don't know."

I'm still sawing. "Don't know about what?"

"Kammie's a stripper and a whore."

"But it don't matter," I say, sounding like I'm an expert on matters of the heart, which I most certainly am not. The only thing I know about the heart is that it makes a nasty mess when you're cutting someone up. "If you love her, that's all that matters."

Cutter pauses, considering this. "She's been with a lot of guys though. She's a fuckin' whore for chrissake!"

"Ain't none of 'em virgins, Cutter."

He grins. "Well, some of the ones Sammy fucks are."

We both chuckle. I look at him again. "Think of it this way," I say. "Suppose you get with her and she's fucked a couple hundred guys, one or two times apiece." I see him wince at this, so I speed to the next part. "Okay, so instead of her you get with sweet Judy, the good girl down the block. She's only been with three guys."

"I don't follow."

"But sweet Judy has been in a serious relationship with each of those guys," I say. "So, she's only fucked three guys, but she's fucked each of them five hundred times." I look at him and say, "Which one is better?"

"That's a good question," he says, pondering this. "It's a trade-off.

42

She's been with less guys, but she's been fucked a whole lot more, so her pussy is all used up." He looks at me and says, "I don't think either one of those options are all that good."

I do a half-shrug with my shoulders as I'm still hunkered down over Jake. "It is what it is."

Cutter stands there for a few minutes, watching me saw. "How about you? You ever been in love?"

I think about this for a moment before answering. "I thought I was once, but that didn't work out. She fucked a bunch of guys and lied a lot. Gave me the clap."

"Was that the one you got the kid with?"

"Nah. This was a couple jumps back." I look at Cutter. "But you know what?"

"What?"

"I think I might be in love now."

He stares at me and his eyes grow wide. *"With Linda the dog bitch?"*

"No," I laugh.

"Good! I was startin' to worry about you."

"But this could be worse."

He stares at me, trying to understand. "How could it be worse?"

"I think I'm in love with a girl I've never even gone out with."

"But you've fucked her, right?"

"No, nothing like that," I say. "It's just a girl I like from a distance."

Cutter laughs. He knows who I'm talking about now. "That redhead from the bowling alley," he says. "Look at that—Bonesaw Billy's in love. You should cut that into a tree somewhere: 'Billy loves...'" He looks at me and says, "What's her name?"

"Grace," I tell him. "And when I cut that into a tree, you can scrawl Cutter loves Kammie on a stripper pole."

He looks at me indignantly for a moment and then shrugs. "So what? She's a stripper and a whore. At least we know she can fuck."

"Bullshit," I say. "I've been with a lot of whores who couldn't fuck if their lives depended on it."

One of them was Kammie, who just laid there as still as the body I'm sawing, but I don't mention this to Cutter. This was back when she first started at the Booby Trap, before Cutter had even met her. I could tell him, sure, and he'd walk away from her in a heartbeat. But I wouldn't do that because it would break his heart.

"Seriously, man," I say. "You gotta promise not to tell anybody about Grace."

Cutter makes the cross sign over his chest. "Cross my heart and all that good goddamn I-love-Jesus bullshit."

"Thanks," I say. "Now dig the fuckin' hole."

FOURTEEN

CRACKER JACK, Cutter, and me show up for our meeting with Reverend Sammy and the cop about forty-five minutes early. We're inside the First Redeemer Church of Branson, and Sammy is speaking to his congregation. I've never seen a minister preach dressed like him; the fucking guy's wearing a blue Fila track suit that's half unzipped, with only his hairy chest and a gold necklace underneath. He's got a pair of sunglasses sitting atop his head and he's wearing camo crocs. He's crying and talking about sin. Seeing this charade makes me laugh since I've seen him commit more sins and do more debauched shit to bus station skanks than I can even begin to remember. Then there's the murders, torture, and violence. He's at the front of the church laying it on thick, explaining that the wages of sin are death. Maybe all those poor bastards Sammy's killed had it coming, I think. Maybe he's just been doing the Lord's work all this time. This thought makes me chuckle under my breath.

When the service is over, the three of us hang back, watching Sammy shake hands with all the holier-than-thou do-gooders, none of whom have the slightest idea what kind of scumbag fuck he really is. Once all the handshaking and "how's your family" chitchat has concluded, he walks over and puts his arm around Cracker Jack. He looks at me. "So, what did you think, Bill? Did you learn anything?"

Yeah, I think. I learned that you're an even bigger piece of shit than I realized. Of course, I don't say that. "I mighta learned a little."

He looks at me skeptically. "Like what?"

I'm drawing a blank. "I don't know, boss. I'm not good at retaining information. If I'd known there was gonna be a test, I woulda taken notes."

He stares at me for a moment, trying to decide whether I'm being a smartass. He finally decides I'm not. Meanwhile, Cutter is yap, yap, yapping about being the caboose when he and some guys were running a train on an old lady from Lampe, but I'm trying not to listen. I look up at one of the stained glass windows where there's a colorful image of Jesus looking down happily, and I think about him looking down at Cutter as he describes how he fucked and took a piss on someone's grandma.

Cutter stops talking. I turn and see the two cops walking in.

"I see you brought backup," Cracker Jack says.

Before Grissom can respond, Sammy says, "You was supposed to come alone."

"Nobody said that," Grissom says.

"It was implied."

Grissom holds his palms up. "He's here now. What do you want me to do?"

"Have him wait in the fuckin' car," I say.

Grissom levels his gaze at me. "He stays or I walk."

Cracker Jack and Sammy exchange looks, and Cutter says, "The nerve of this fuckin' pig."

Sammy dismisses it. "Whatever. Let the coon stay. Come on, follow me into the fellowship hall." He turns and heads there, but Marshall says, *"I ain't no coon!"* Sammy spins around and points at him. "Let's get this straight," he says, "you're both pieces of garbage. Call yourselves whatever you like, I don't care. Tomato, tomahto, you're both a couple of chuckle-fucks." Then he turns and leads the way.

As we walk into the fellowship hall, Grissom says, "I've never heard of a chuckle-fuck." I hear Sammy groan and he shakes his head, but he doesn't comment. He leads us to a succession of connected folding tables. We all sit. I see an image in my mind of the last supper, only instead of Jesus holding court it's Sammy's fat ass.

Grissom turns to Sammy. "Cracker Jack told you? About my sister and the safe and all that?"

Instead of answering, Sammy produces a pill bottle from his pocket. He unscrews the cap and spills a couple Oxys onto the table. Then he uses the bottom of the bottle to crush the pills. Once the Oxys are powder, Sammy leans down and snorts it. This whole process takes about two minutes, and no one says a word the entire time. Everyone just watches, waiting for him to speak.

Finally, he looks up with watery eyes. "Cracker Jack told me."

"Okay," Grissom says. "So whaddaya think?"

"I think you're a worthless rat fuck."

The cops' expressions are priceless, and I can see that Cutter is having a hard time keeping a straight face.

"There's no reason to talk to us like that," Marshall says.

Sammy shrugs. "No one cares what you think. You think I give a nickel dick butt plug what you think?

"I don't even know what that means," Grissom says, annoyed. "So, are we gonna do this or not?"

Sammy stares at him with a very intense, solemn stare. "I hear your wife is a real looker, Grissom."

Grissom wasn't expecting this, and he looks startled. He looks around at everyone's faces, trying to read the room, but we're all as stoic as Abraham Lincoln watching the play.

"*What?*" he manages.

"You heard me," Sammy says. "The boys told me you got a cute wife with big ol' titties and fat dick-sucker lips."

We laugh. The cops don't.

"What the hell?" Grissom asks, his cheeks as red as a blood-soaked tampon.

Sammy leans forward, staring at him. "The way I see it, there's two ways we can go here."

"I'd like to hear 'em," Grissom says.

Sammy pulls a Glock nine out from under the table, and I wonder where the hell he was hiding it during his sermon. He's holding it flat against the table top. "The first is, we can plug a couple bullets in both of your heads and go get the money ourselves... Then we don't have to share a dime with you or your whore sister."

Grissom looks pissed. "I wouldn't give you the code."

Cracker Jack explodes with laughter. Grissom turns to find out what's funny. When he does, Cracker Jack cracks his knuckles. "Trust me, you'll give it up. They always give it up. It's like the Nazis in those old war movies, *'vee have vays of making you talk'*."

The cops look nervous and about a hundred beads of sweat appear on Grissom's forehead.

"Okay," Grissom says. "What's the second option?"

Sammy grins. "I get to buttfuck your wife."

Again, we all laugh, but the cops don't.

"Is that some kinda joke?" Grissom asks, his voice wavering.

"Reverend Sammy don't joke around," Cutter says. "If he tells you he's gonna buttfuck your wife, consider that bitch buttfucked."

Riding the momentum of the moment, I grin big and say, "He might even buttfuck her in the face!" I'm not sure what this line even means, but it sounds funny and it gets a big laugh from everyone who's not a cop.

Sammy still has the gun lying flat against the table. He turns it towards Grissom and grins. "I think I might fuck her with my Glock, pig. What you think about that?"

Grissom stares at him in horror. "What are you saying?"

Cutter says, "You know."

Sammy sits back and says matter-of-factly, "We're gonna take turns raping her. You can fight and die, or you can just let it happen. It's your choice."

Grissom looks terrified and he starts to tremble. He looks at Sammy with big, scared, glassy eyes. In that moment, the look on his face tells us he's already resigned himself and his wife to their fate. "Okay," he says as he starts to sob. "I guess you can..." He takes a breath before finishing. "Fuck her. Just... don't hurt her."

Sammy stares at him coldly for a long moment. Then, finally, he smiles and says, "I'm just fuckin' with you, pig. But thanks for the offer."

Everyone laughs and the humiliated cop lets out a sigh of relief. Then he laughs too, pretending he was in on the joke. But he wasn't. And in this moment, I realize how beautiful a move this was on Sammy's part. This was a power play. After this, Sammy has established himself as the one in control, and no one dares challenge him after that.

FIFTEEN

It's Wednesday night at Funland, and the place is lit up in all its decadent glory. It pissed rain for a bit, but now there's only a light mist. Apparently, nobody gives a fuck though because the park is packed. The beauty of Funland is, thanks to the tourists, it's busy as hell almost every day it's open.

Music is playing, rides are twirling, and everyone's having a good time. I'm sitting on my perch wearing clown makeup in the dunk tank, doing what I do best—making people mad. In these past few months, I've established that I'm as good as old Ray was, maybe better. I like the job, although my throat hurts most of the time from the constant yelling, so sometimes I talk like an old hag who smokes a hundred Marlboros a day. But tonight, I've my full voice.

I'm chiding a one-armed man, making cracks about him trying to shop in a secondhand store—you know, the normal shit—when I notice Grace and her cop boyfriend coming down the fairway. He's wearing a blue polo, so I don't know for certain he's the cop boyfriend as I've never seen him, but... well, yes, I do. I do because cops only come in one model. They all have steely eyes and square jaws. Mirror sunglasses sitting on top of short hair. Smirks at the corners of their mouths like they've got the biggest dicks in the place. They all look like guys who lift weights but don't do cardio. Instead they sit in their cruisers and eat Krispy Kremes all day. Their chests are puffed out 24/7 because they've got something to prove. This is why they became cops in the first place. Somebody pissed in their Cheerios when they were kids, so now they take out their anger on everyone else. The easiest way to spot a cop in plainclothes is to look for the giant chip on his shoulder.

Even though the one-armed crip is up front chucking baseballs, I've grown tired of him. With my eyes on Grace's boyfriend I say, "Why don't you give it up, pal, and let someone else have a try? *Someone like that pig cop back there!*" I say it loud and the cop hears it. His little piggy ears perk up and he looks in my direction. I can tell Grace didn't hear it, but he did. His ears are used to hearing everyone snickering and calling him shit like "pig" and "five-oh" everywhere he goes. He's got piggy radar, so he's attuned to that.

He's looking at me when I point at him. *"Yeah, you, you pig fuck! The one with the girl who's way too cute for your stupid pig ass!"* The dumb bastard is standing there with his chest puffed out a little extra now, and he's turning red. He's confused and unsure what to do, making me thankful I'm not an unarmed black man because we all know what would happen in that scenario. *"You shoot any innocent people today, Kojak?!"* He points at me and says something, but I can't hear him. I'm the one with a microphone, so fuck him. This is my show.

Grace is watching now, and the cop wants to look tough for her, so he's walking towards the throw line. The ever-growing crowd is watching to see what he'll do, and the one-armed crip hands him the ball. My assistant Chuck tells him it's two dollars for three throws. The cop grimaces. Most cops are on the take and make good money, but they're all cheap and hate to give up a buck. Seeing a cop part with his money is almost as rare as seeing Moses part the Red Sea. But this fucker is good and pissed, so he forks the money over.

I pile on like a fumble at the five. *"Show us that arm of yours, Porky Pig! Show us what you got!"*

He reaches back and hurls the ball, but it falls short, striking the wall beneath the sensor. I laugh and, to my surprise, everyone else laughs too. A macho fuck like him hates being mocked.

Now I really lay it on. "Blue Lives Matter?" I say, laughing. *"Blue Lives Murder!"* There's a collective gasp from the crowd, but no one is more shocked than he is. He points at me and yells, *"Fuck you!"* He actually screams it loud enough that I can hear it this time. I laugh hard and say, "Isn't that disorderly conduct? Disturbing the peace maybe? Way to set an example, Barney Fife!" He gets even angrier and hurls ball number two, which is not only short but wide to the left, completely missing the entire wall. Everyone laughs again, louder now.

The cop stands there with egg on his face, embarrassed and angry. He's as red as a beet dipped in ketchup and he looks as if his head might explode at any second. He points at me and yells, *"Watch yourself!"* I laugh. The moron doesn't even take the third ball. He stalks back to Grace and I see him grab her arm. She takes one last look at me and I wonder if she recognizes me in clown face. Even though her boyfriend is turned away, I give a little wave, more for her benefit than his. *"So long, pig!"*

Pleased with myself, I go back to yelling at the other losers. I'm feeling particularly mean-spirited now, so I dig deep and really let them have it. I'm talking about their dead mothers and their ugly wives. I even make one fucker cry. I'm not sure why I'm doing this. Probably because I hate seeing Grace with another man.

The rest of the night passes quickly and closing time comes. The fairway is mostly empty, and the lights are coming down one by one. I'm climbing out from the tank and all I can think about is how tired I am and how much I want a beer. My back is turned when I hear Chuck yell, *"Watch out, Billy!"* I turn around just in time to see the cop's fist a millisecond before it smashes into my face. I fall to the ground, trying to make sense of it. I look up at the dumb bastard and try to shake away the stars in my eyes.

"*You thought you were pretty funny up there tonight, didn't you?*" he asks. I'm still trying to get my head straight. The cop steps forward and kicks me hard in the ribs and pain shoots through my body. He growls, "*How did you even know I was a cop?*" I look up at him and smile with bloody teeth. "It's because you look like a fag."

He steps towards me so he can kick me again, but I see something come down on top of his head. I sit up a little, watching him crumple to the ground like a wad of used paper. Now I see Cracker Jack standing there with a pipe wrench. He's looking down at the cop and he starts to scream. "*There you go, you dumbfuck! That's what you get! You wanna play stupid games, you win stupid prizes!*" But the cop doesn't hear any of this because he's out for the count.

I rise to my feet and shake my head again, trying to get it straight. I see Grace standing about ten feet away. She's staring at me with a confused expression. I speak to her. "Grace?" My words bring her to life, and she says, "I thought that was you." She comes towards me. My hands are trembling as I pull out my smokes and light one. She's right in front of me now, staring at me with those big green eyes. "You look gorgeous," I say. She smiles and we kiss, our shadows looming over her unconscious boyfriend.

Scratch that. *Ex*-boyfriend.

SIXTEEN

BEING part of the Funland crew is amazing. These are the best days of my life.

When I was growing up in the decrepit older-than-God aluminum trailer in a Shreveport trailer park that was seedy even by trailer park standards, I dreamed of being a basketball player someday. I had posters and cut-out magazine photos of Michael Jordan tacked to the wood-panel walls in my bedroom. I used to look up at those and imagine myself playing in the NBA and doing the kinds of on-court heroics MJ did. I might have accomplished that dream had it not been for the fact that my basketball skills are roughly the same as those of a quadriplegic dwarf with Downs.

My sperm-donor dad ran out on us when I was three. It was that same old "went out for a pack of smokes and never came back" bullshit, except in my old man's case it was crack. I only have one memory of him and that's riding with him on his Harley. That's a good memory, but I think it's one my mind made up to make me feel better about my dad being a piece of shit. I have no way of knowing if it's true. I would ask my mom, but she got herself killed by one of her johns one evening while I was playing outside. The fucker slit her

54

throat so wide and so deep her head almost came off. I was eight. That was a truly horrific experience. I was the one who found her lying there covered in blood. That's an image I've never forgotten. In fact, I still have nightmares about it.

After my mother was killed, no one would take me in except my Uncle Boyd, who sold pot and had a taste for molesting little boys. He eventually got himself locked up for it, but not until after he'd destroyed my childhood just a little more.

I got arrested for the first time when I was twelve. What happened was, I had this old hag of a science teacher who had it in for me. She kept mouthing off, telling me not to talk or carve pictures of dicks and titties on my desk. Finally, she mouthed off one too many times and I hauled off and socked her. I got in deep shit, but I also broke her jaw. I've always been proud of that. So, I went off to juvie for a while, where I learned all kinds of criminal shit. I hadn't been learning much at school, but behind bars I learned a lot. I was a fucking straight A student when it came to crime. So, when I got out, I was doing all kinds of wild shit like stealing cars and stealing... well, stealing everything I could get my hands on. If it wasn't nailed down, I stole it. I got a rush whenever I'd steal something. It eventually got to the point where I was stealing shit I didn't even want just for the thrill of doing it.

I went to juvie again when I was sixteen. This time I helped some friends rob a house. My friend Jimmy, who was this badass black kid who sold dope, took a bunch of us to this teacher's house so he could fuck her. She said we could watch TV or help ourselves to some snacks while Jimmy was pounding her in the next room. Instead, we stole everything from the TV to the DVD player to the fucking microwave. When they got finished fucking, the teacher came out to find all her stuff missing. This chick didn't wanna call the cops on account of her being a teacher screwing a minor, so she sent her ex-husband to track us down and retrieve her stuff. When the guy showed up at my uncle's place, I decided to take batting practice with the new aluminum baseball bat I'd stolen from Walmart.

After that, I did stupid shit here and there, like beating up people for money or delivering packages for a drug dealer. One of those packages went all the way to St. Louis. I ended up staying in St. Louis and eventually came to work at Funland.

When I told Sammy I loved committing crime, I wasn't shitting him. I enjoy doing all kinds of crimes. If it's illegal, I'll do it; everything from parking in handicap parking spots to armed robbery to busting heads. And you know what? I still get the same rush I did when I started. Drugs eventually lose their edge after you've done them for a while, but not crime. At least not for me.

All my friends are here at Funland. I've got a lot of friends, such as Randy, who operates a dart game where suckers win AC/DC mirrors on prize row, and Harry, the old black man who can make his eyes pop out as part of the freak show. But mostly I just stick close to Cracker Jack and Cutter, just like I did when I first started. I look up to Cracker Jack. He's a hard man who doesn't take any shit, but he's loyal if he likes you. Lucky for me, he loves me. And whenever I have a question regarding some type of criminal activity, he always has the answer. Cracker Jack is a fucking how-to-do-crimes encyclopedia.

And Cutter... I love Cutter like the brother I never wanted. Sometimes he does ignorant shit and gets out of hand. He's got the shortest fuse I've ever seen, but I'd do anything for him. And I know I can count on him if I ever need him. Cutter loves Kammie, the stripper from the Booby Trap, and I honestly think he's gonna pop the question soon. I can't imagine him as a married man, but I'm happy for him if he thinks it will make him happy.

I'm good with Sammy, but I don't trust him any further than I can throw Marvin the 600-pound man. Sammy has always been good to me, and I think he genuinely likes me. I want to like him, but I'm smart enough to see him for the snake he is. Cutter feels the same way and has voiced this opinion on multiple occasions. I think Cracker Jack probably feels this way too, but he's extremely loyal and has never said much about him. And Cutter and I know enough not to ask.

I don't mind working in the dunk tank, but it gets hotter than two eighteen-year-old lesbians with double Ds going down on each other in a sauna. But really, I'm just here for the crime. I'm here to be part of a family. I never had one at home, but here I do. I'm part of something, even if it's a white trash crime family.

SEVENTEEN

ME AND THIS weirdo named Deuce Clemons are watching Cutter play the Kiss pinball machine at the Bowl-Mor. Deuce has this weird build where his top half looks as round as a tomato, but his legs are as skinny as toothpicks. He's a flabby fucker and he wears cutoff muscle shirts, exposing the faded Woody Woodpecker tat on his bicep. He's got a crooked goatee and a confederate flag doo-rag he's probably worn every day since he dropped out of high school thirty years ago. He's a harmless goofball who works as the Bowl-Mor janitor and handyman. Cutter and I have often wondered how he got the job. My guess is he's one of Sammy's relatives. He, he might even be Bella's dad. Cutter enjoys giving him a hard time and he purposely calls him "Douche" instead of Deuce, pretending he doesn't know how to pronounce it. Deuce always gets really flustered and watching that never gets old.

It's late and the Sunday night crowd is thinning. Deuce and I are watching Cutter play, and Cutter is telling us about a girl he knew in high school who would let him and the other boys do nasty shit to her in exchange for CDs. "She had the best CD collection in the school," he says, chuckling.

"Was she cute?" Deuce asks.

"Christ no," Cutter says. "She looked kinda like Tony the concession guy, except with slightly smaller tits." He laughs and we laugh with him. Cutter loves being the center of attention and telling stories about his sexploits. I don't believe most of them, but they're still entertaining. Cutter's vocabulary is fairly limited, but he can tell a story like nobody's business.

After Cutter loses his pinball, he stops to tell his story. Deuce and I are flanking him, so he looks back and forth as he talks. "One Friday I go over there, I say, 'Listen Tina, I ain't got no money this week, but I still want some ass!" He chuckles. "So she says, 'Maybe we can work out a deal.' I say, 'Oh yeah? What kinda deal?'" He pauses, looking at us for effect. "She says, 'I got my period.' I say, 'Okay, no big deal, we've fucked on your period before.' But she says, 'No. That's not it. I been thinkin'.' I say, 'Yeah? What are you thinking about?' She says, 'Well, I fantasize all the time about having a guy get down and eat my pussy while I'm on the rag.' I say, 'Oh yeah? That's what you want?' She says, 'Maybe you can do that for me and in return I'll fuck you.'"

Cutter looks back and forth at us again.

"So, what did you do?" asks Deuce.

I know Cutter like I know the back of my hand, so I already know.

"Well," Cutter says, beaming, "I ate her bloody snatch."

"You're a nasty motherfucker," I say.

Cutter laughs proudly, basking in the attention.

"That's disgusting," Deuce says. "What did it taste like?"

"It wasn't too bad. Not much different than usual, except a little bit saltier. But unless you got high blood pressure, who gives a shit? It's just salt."

I tell Cutter he's a sick fuck, which makes him chuckle. He doubles down and really goes for it. "I had blood streaks on both of my cheeks," he says, pointing at his face. "That was the night I got my... uh..." Cutter is thinking, trying to remember the term. "I got my... uh... you know..." He's still searching for the word when Deuce pipes up and says, *"Red wings! You got your red wings!"*

Cutter frowns and turns towards Deuce. "What the fuck did you say?" His tone is weirdly angry. I can't see his eyes from where I'm standing, but I know there's fire in them. Deuce's eyes get big and he tries to explain. "That's what they call it, Cutter! They call it getting your red wings!"

Cutter is so angry you can almost see steam coming out of his ears. He's trembling. Cutter screams, *"Motherfucker!"* He lunges towards Deuce. Deuce's eyes are open wide, so he gets a real good look at Cutter's fist when Cutter punches him in the eye. Before Deuce is even on the floor, Cutter is on top of him, beating him.

"Hey, hey," I say. I move forward and grab Cutter's arm, trying to pull him off. Cutter turns and glares at me. *"Leave me the fuck alone!"* I tell him no. After all, he's got no reason to be mad. Once I've got Cutter pulled off Deuce, I help Deuce stand. Deuce's eye and cheek are swollen fatter than a Kardashian's ass. "Are you okay?" I ask. Deuce nods, looking confused, not knowing what just happened. "I think so," he says. I put my hand on his back, trying to console him.

No one else in the place is even looking our way. At Funland, no one's surprised by anything. So, they go on with their business, chatting or doing blow or bowling or whatever the fuck they're doing. I think back to Cracker Jack's advice about not fucking with anyone at the Bowl-Mor. Apparently this rule doesn't apply to Deuce.

Cutter must be feeling bad because he apologizes. "Look, Deuce, I'm sorry. I shouldn't have done that."

Deuce looks at him with a wary expression. "You finally said my name right."

"Will ya shut up already?" Cutter says. "I'm tryin' to apologize, ya prick. I was out of line. Let me fix this."

I have no idea what Cutter is doing. I love Cutter, but I've never seen him act nice to anyone outside our immediate circle. No one without a pussy anyway.

"Come outside," Cutter says. "I've got something in my car. When you see this..." Cutter chuckles, his eyes twinkling. "When I fuck up, I'm not afraid to admit it." This is interesting because I've never seen Cutter apologize even once, ever. But he's doing it now. He's actually trying to make amends. "Let's go outside. I wanna give you something. When you see it, you'll understand what I'm talking about. I just got my hands on it myself, and it's worth a small fortune. It won't make your eye feel any better, and I'm sorry for that, but it's the best I can do."

Deuce is staring at him with a dopey, confused expression.

"Just come on," Cutter says, grinning big. "You'll see." He looks at me. "You'll *both* see!"

The three of us walk outside and make our way towards Cutter's Caddy. "How's your face feel?" Cutter asks.

"Not too good, to tell you the truth," Deuce says.

"I'm really fucking sorry. I don't know what came over me. And to be honest, my hand don't feel too good neither. But I've got something that's gonna smooth this all over, Deuce. I promise you, you're gonna love it."

The two of them are friendly now and I wonder what Cutter's gonna give him.

Deuce looks over at him as we near the car. "What is it?"

Cutter grins. "I don't wanna ruin the surprise."

The two of them are walking in front of me, and I'm just listening. When Cutter gets to the trunk, he unlocks it. Then he tells Deuce to come over to the trunk and look inside. Deuce does.

"What am I supposed to see?" Deuce asks.

"Lean in and look closer," Cutter says. "You'll see it."

Deuce pauses before leaning into the trunk. When he finally does, Cutter reaches up and grabs the trunk lid, smashing it down onto Deuce's back. Deuce lets out a howl and Cutter says, *"I'll teach you to fucking correct me, you motherfucker!"* Free from the trunk, Deuce drops to the pavement. Cutter steps back and kicks him in the face like he's kicking a field goal, and Deuce flops backwards. Cutter walks around him, kicking him in the face again, and Deuce is unconscious.

Cutter takes one last look at his handiwork and turns around, closing the trunk. Then he sits on top of it and says, "You believe the nerve of this guy?"

I sit on the trunk beside him. "He didn't do anything."

"That fucker did a lot. He shoulda never corrected me."

I tell him that's not the way I saw it.

Cutter stares at the bowling alley. "Maybe, maybe not. I dunno. Could be I overreacted."

"Could be," I say.

Cutter turns towards me and says, "I got something to tell you."

"That you wanna fuck me?"

Cutter doesn't laugh. His expression is as serious as a mortician's.

"Okay," I say. "What?"

"Kammie."

"What about her?"

Cutter meets my gaze. "I wanna marry her."

"I knew you would."

He looks at me with a pissy expression. "You don't know shit."

"I knew," I say. "But so what?"

"I haven't asked her yet, but I wanna do some fancy shit, like maybe take her to Olive Garden or have Toby Keith come and meet her."

"You like Toby Keith?" I ask.

"Fuck no. I don't listen to that fag stuff. But Kammie likes him."

"Fair enough," I say.

"Maybe I'll have Toby Keith ask her to marry me."

"How you gonna get a hold of Toby Keith?"

"I dunno," he says. "Maybe I'll ask some other way, but I'm gonna ask."

"That sounds good."

"But here's the thing, Bill. I want you to be the best man."

I stare at him, slightly surprised. No one has ever asked me to be a part of anything special. Even when my ex had the baby, she asked me not to be there. "Sure, Cutter," I say. "I'll do that."

I've never had a brother before, but I realize in this moment that Cutter absolutely is my brother.

"Congratulations," I say. And for the first time ever, Cutter doesn't make a wisecrack. He just hugs me and says, "Thanks, man."

EIGHTEEN

It's our first date and Grace invites me to her place for dinner and a movie. She greets me at the door with a smile. We don't kiss and I'm wondering if we're going to pretend we haven't kissed already. But the night is young, and the date being at her house is a good sign. The food she's cooking smells terrific, and she informs me she's got "three cheese baked pasta" in the oven. She asks, "Do you like cheese?" I laugh and say, "More than R. Kelly loves pissing on kids." She laughs.

We sit on the couch as the pasta bakes. Grace scrolls through Netflix trying to find something for us to watch. I'm curious what movie she's gonna pick. A movie tells you a lot about a person.

This is what I know about her beyond her being gorgeous: She carries herself confidently, but then why wouldn't she be? She looks like a million bucks. She's got great tits. That's probably not the most important thing, but I'd be lying if I said I didn't think about it. I know she's classier than me. I can tell she comes from a lower-class background that's still ten miles above the Florida trailer park I come from. She looks like a girl who probably wore Hot Topic, where I wore my cousins' Dollar Store hand-me-downs. I don't give a shit about Hot Topic, but the only way I could have worn those clothes was if I'd stolen them. But she's not some hoity-toity stuck-up bitch; she just comes from better stock than my deadbeat dad and murdered whore mother. Because of this, I wonder if we have any chance at an actual relationship. I'll gladly take the one- or two-time fuck if that's what this is, but I want something real.

"Is this okay?" she asks, pointing to *Fight Club*. "Excellent choice," I say. The discovery that she's got good taste makes me happy, and no matter what happens, I know I'm not going to be forced to suffer through *The Notebook*, which I have done before for a piece of ass.

She meets my gaze. "You've seen it?"

"A time or twelve, yeah."

"You're sure it's okay?"

"Totally okay." She's turned towards me now and I'm looking into those beautiful green eyes. I know this sounds like some *Notebook* shit, but I could get lost in them. She likes me, and I can see it on her face which pleases me. She asks, "Where would you like this to end up?"

This startles me and I blush. "Do you mean long-term or just tonight?"

"Slow down, hoss," she says, giggling. "I meant this date."

There are two ways I can answer her. One, I could say the romantic thing like *Romeo and Juliet* or whatever, or two, I could say something dirty and flirty. I wonder which of these responses will play better. Fuck it, I think. I've gotta be me, so I go the Billy Hanson route. "With me waking up in the morning, picking your pubes out of my teeth."

Her expression changes to one of shock and she gasps, so I'm hoping I didn't fuck this up before it's even begun. But then she erupts into laughter and I realize it's going to be okay. "That's what you want, huh?" Before I can answer, she leans in and we kiss. This goes on for about ten minutes and she's got the greatest lips. I kind of doubt that we're gonna get to either *Fight Club* or the pasta, which is a shame because it smells amazing. Everything is going great and I've got my hand up the back of her shirt. Everything is hot and heavy when we're interrupted by a knock at the door. Grace frowns. "I'll be right back," she whispers as she gets up to answer it.

Grace opens the door and it's the cop.

"Who's here, Grace?" he asks.

"What makes you think someone is here?"

"I saw the Caddy out front," he says. "It's registered to a Manny Dominguez."

That's Cutter's real name. I sit silently on the couch as this plays out.

"Jeremy," she says, "you shouldn't be here. I told you I don't want to see you anymore."

He disregards her. "Let me talk to him."

"Jeremy."

"Let me talk to him," he repeats.

Now this cock-blocker is starting to piss me off. I stand and go to the door, looking out at the uniformed pig, standing there in the light rain. I smirk and nod. "Hi." He reads the mocking tone of my voice. It's one thing cops recognize and hate. He says, "You don't look like a Manny Dominguez."

"Well," I say, "you don't look like a tough guy."

His demeanor switches from annoyance to anger.

"Do I know you?" he asks.

"No, but your mama does."

He glares at me. "Alright, come outside, pal."

I smile big, trying to look like I don't care, and I move past Grace and step out into the rain. His hand is on his gun. "Turn around and face the doorway."

"What the hell?" I ask.

"*Fucking do it!*" You've gotta love cops. They've got the thinnest skins and they go from ten to one-twenty in a millisecond. I turn around and the fucker cuffs me, making a point to tighten the cuffs way too tight. He reads me my rights.

"*What the hell, Jeremy?*" Grace says.

"This is a bad look," I say. "You can't please Grace, so you're taking it out on me."

I can't see Jeremy's face, but I know his type and I know these comments are like daggers in his chest. He puts his arm around me and leads me through the rain to his cruiser.

"Please don't do this!" Grace yells behind us. Jeremy doesn't say a word.

When we get to the car, he opens the back door and pushes me in. I'm shocked he doesn't bang my head on the top of the car as he does. That's an old favorite from the cop playbook. They like to show you how tough they are while your hands are restrained, and you can't do anything.

I'm in the back of the car, and I'm sitting on my cuffed hands, growing angrier by the second. I've done this a million times and it never ceases to piss me off. But this, this is different.

We're on our way to the station now, and I can't help myself. Jeremy hasn't figured out who I am, and I want him to know. I *need* him to know. I say in my mocking clown voice, *"Hey there, piggy, piggy, remember me?"* He cocks his head a little and I can see the wheels turning. "Blue Lives Matter?" I say. "Blue Lives Murder!" I laugh hard and I can see he's made the connection. His jerky mannerisms make it as obvious as if a cartoon light bulb had suddenly appeared over his head.

"I got something for you, dipshit," he growls.

I know saying this is a bad idea, but I do it anyway. "That's a shock since it seems you didn't have anything to give Grace."

He chuckles, and I know I'm in for some real shit now. I might not live through the night. I don't want to die, but in the grand scheme of things I feel like I'm a winner because I've pushed his buttons.

NINETEEN

Jeremy drives me out of Branson and into the country. He's still laughing and talking shit when we turn onto a gravel road. He looks at me in the rearview. "You keep flapping that mouth of yours, you're liable to get something stuck in it." He's staring at me to see if I'm scared. I *am* scared—who the fuck wouldn't be? But I refuse to let him see it.

"It won't be much," I say, winking at him in the mirror. "Not according to Grace."

This is, of course, a lie, but he doesn't know that. The glee in his eyes disappears and it's immediately replaced with anger.

"We'll see what you're made of, shit for brains," he says.

My gaze is level, and my fear gives way to sheer unadulterated anger. I want to take my anger out on his face. "Why don't you take these cuffs off of me and we'll see who wins, pig."

He looks back at the road. "Keep on talkin', smart guy."

"Smarter than you."

He looks at me in the rearview again. "I'll bet you didn't even graduate high school."

Without flinching I say, "I was smart enough not to become a

68

fucking cop." His gaze holds on me in that mirror for a long moment. I add, "I must be doing something right seeing how I'm the one fucking Grace now."

He turns back towards the road and I wonder if I've gone too far. I wonder if he's going to kill me. I can't stand the silence, so I double down. I tell him about his mother, his tiny pecker, everything bad I can think of to say about cops, and tons of other awful, infuriating shit, but he just keeps looking ahead at the gravel road.

Finally, after we've been driving for a while, Jeremy pulls into the driveway of a decrepit, abandoned house. He looks at me in the rearview. "You ready, boy?"

He gets out into the rain and comes to the rear door. He opens it, reaching in and grabbing me by my shirt. I wiggle and yell. *"This isn't fair!"*

"It ain't supposed to be."

He pulls me out into the rain and onto my feet. I wobble a little, and he delivers a hard uppercut into my stomach, which hurts and takes my breath away. I keel over for a moment. Then I straighten and look at him. "That all you got?" He hits me again, the exact same punch in the exact same place. Jeremy is stronger than I imagined, and the uppercuts hurt like a sonofabitch. I'm doubled over in pain when the third uppercut comes up from under me, catching me in the eye.

He's wearing a ring, and Jesus, it hurts something awful. I flop back against the car, my handcuffed hands between me and the door. I'm trying to clear my eyes when Jeremy punches me in the nose. It breaks. I feel and hear it crack. Within seconds, I taste salty blood on my lips.

Jeremy is standing there lording over me with a big grin. "You ain't so funny now, are you, boy?"

I manage to open my eyes to a squint, looking him in his eyes. "Not as funny as your tiny dick." This sets him off again, delivering blow after blow to my abdomen and jaw. One of his punches hits me in the side of my throat. I'm not sure if he meant to do that, but it hurts like holy hell and I have a hard time catching my breath.

I'm face down on the gravel driveway now, and Jeremy is kicking me in the ribs, and again I can feel and hear them break.

"How you like that, you dumb shit?!" he yells.

I lie with my arms behind my back, silent. My entire body hurts. I open my mouth a little and I taste gravel. He starts kicking me again. And again. And again.

Everything goes black.

TWENTY

I'M OUTSIDE in the warm sun. I can't see myself, but somehow, I'm aware that I'm a child. I'm swinging a stick, sword fighting an imaginary opponent. I do this for a few moments, but I'm thirsty and decide to go inside for a drink. I turn towards the trailer and walk to the steps. I go up them and open the door to the trailer. When I do, I see her—my mother, lying there, covered in blood. I want to scream, but I can't. As I'm staring at the slab of meat that used to be my mother, I see her move. Maybe she's okay, I think, knowing she isn't. She turns her head. The gash on her neck is huge and her head doesn't seem to be attached correctly, but she still manages to look at me. Her bloody face grins. "You always were a fuck up, Billy."

I startle awake, and it all comes back. I'm lying face down in the gravel driveway. My body hurts worse than it has ever hurt before. The pain is everywhere, all at once. My head is pounding, my busted nose hurts, my ribs hurt, my stomach hurts. Thankfully, my hands aren't cuffed anymore. I can't muster the energy to stand, so I just turn my head towards the road. The earliest signs of morning are starting to show. Jeremy and his cop car are long gone. I close my eyes and drift off to sleep again.

When I wake up again, I'm lying in a bed in Cox Medical. I blink my eyes and squint, trying to clear my vision. When I do, I see Cracker Jack standing there rubbing his hands, looking angry.

"There he is," I hear Cutter say. I look over and see him sitting in the room's only chair.

"How the fuck did I get here?" I ask, trying to work it out. Almost as soon as the words leave my mouth, I remember that fuckhead Jeremy kicking my ass.

Cracker Jack looks at me with a confused look. "That's what we were gonna ask you."

"Never mind," I say. "I remember now. I got worked over by that stupid cop."

Cracker Jack's face tightens, his head tilts, and his eyes go wild. *"The motherfucker from the other night?"*

"Yeah, but I don't want anything done to him. Not yet. I'll deal with him in my own time."

His eyes narrow. "You don't want us to go get him?"

"He's seeing that girl," Cutter says. "He don't wanna fuck it up."

"That's right," I say. "I like her more than I hate him."

Cracker Jack looks irritated and I can see that he doesn't approve. Why the fuck is *he* irritated? I'm the one who got his head and ribs kicked in. Then he says, "This is about more than just you, kid. When we let somebody do this to a guy in our crew, it makes us all look weak. And we've got guys in the department who can handle him."

Cutter laughs. "We got most of those cop pricks!"

"No," I say. "I'll take care of him."

"When?"

"When it's time," I say. "You've gotta trust me on this. I love you and I respect you, but I'm asking you. Please. Let me handle it."

Cutter says, "If Billy says he's gonna take care of it, he's gonna take care of it. He ain't afraid to get his hands dirty or do what's gotta be done."

Cracker Jack nods, coming around. "I know, I know. Billy always does what needs to be done. But I still don't like it."

"Don't like what?" Cutter asks.

Cracker Jack turns toward him. "This fuckin' cop strolling around out there like he ain't got a care in the world."

"It's okay," I say. "You know me, I'll get him when the time is right. I'll get him good."

"Right!" says Cutter. "He'll get him when the time is right."

"Well," Cracker Jack says, "if you need help, you come to me. I like bustin' heads, especially when it's a cop."

Cutter and I chuckle. We're both well aware of this.

Cracker Jack points at my cheek. "You got marks on your face. Little bitty C's."

"Fancy little C's," Cutter adds.

I nod. "Fucker had a ring on. It musta had a C on it."

Cracker Jack squints at me, trying to understand. "A 'C'? Why a 'C'? His name start with a 'C', or is it just 'C' for cop?"

"His badge said his name was Caparello."

"Italian name," Cutter says.

"Whatever it is, he needs taken care of," Cracker Jack says. "Something he won't walk away from."

I tell him I promise I'll deal with Jeremy. Then I look at Cutter. "I need you to do something for me."

"Anything," he says. "You name it."

"I need you to go find Grace and tell her where I'm at."

TWENTY-ONE

I'M SITTING up in bed watching an episode of *The Andy Griffith Show* when the nurse pops her head in to tell me I have a visitor. Then Grace walks in looking as stunning as ever. She's wearing a *Doctor Who* t-shirt. I don't give a damn about *Doctor Who* and don't know anything about him, but the shirt looks damn good on her. She steps in, carrying a black purse and smiling awkwardly.

"What's a girl like you doing in a place like this?" I ask.

She makes a sad face, and she has tears in her eyes. She apologizes, saying Cutter told her Jeremy did this.

"Don't worry," I say. "It was worth the beating just to see you again."

The line is cheesy, but that's okay. Maybe it's the pain that has me feeling vulnerable, but right now I don't care if it's cheesy. It's true.

Her tough-girl persona is gone. Maybe it's the hospital, maybe it's the fact that her ex put me here for seeing her. She's staring at me awkwardly for a moment, and then she remembers something. "I almost forgot," she says, holding up her purse and searching through it. "I got you something." She pulls out two travel-size bottles of Jack Daniels.

I smile. "Just what the doctor ordered."

"It was the least I could do."

I look into her eyes. "What I really want is to go out with you again."

"We never really got to go out the first time."

"That's true," I say. "I was looking forward to the pasta."

She smirks. "And *Fight Club*."

"Right. *Fight Club*."

"Well," she says, "you said you'd seen it before."

"Of course I have, but that looked like it was gonna be the best viewing of *Fight Club* ever."

She smiles. "You think so?"

"I do." I pause for a moment. "I'd like another chance to watch *Fight Club* with you."

She grins. "There's something about you, Billy."

"I hope it's a good thing."

"It's definitely a good thing," she says. "I don't know how, but I can tell you're not gonna fuck me over." She smirks. "And you strike me as a bit of a player; a guy who's fucked over a girl or two."

I grin. "Maybe. But let me ask you something."

"Okay."

"Did you feel that way about Jeremy? Like he wouldn't fuck you over?"

She shrugs. "Sometimes people make mistakes."

"That guy was definitely a mistake."

We both laugh and she says, "Fuck Jeremy." We laugh again. Then she looks me in the eyes. "Are you sure you're not gonna hurt me?"

"I would never hurt you, Grace."

She leans down and kisses me, and the heart monitor goes wild.

TWENTY-TWO

IT's a Saturday night when we drive to Jeff City to rob Bill White.
The office is on Madison, nestled between a coffee shop and a bar.
The street is bright and fairly well-traveled, even now at eleven. The
bar is called the Black Anchor, and it's on the left. The coffee shop on
the right, Jenny's Java, is closed. The office is plain jane with no
distinguishing markings beyond the words BILL WHITE
CAMPAIGN HEADQUARTERS on the glass door and an askew
VOTE BILL WHITE sign stuck in one of the windows.

There are cars parked along the curb. The first time we drive
past, there are no available spots. But now, after we've dropped
Rahmi, the Funland fortune teller, off in the alley and have come
back, there's an open spot. I park the stolen Honda Odyssey in front
of an insurance agency three store fronts down from the office.

We've got a five-man team. Cracker Jack and Cunny Jaymes are
going inside. Cracker Jack is going to open the safe while Cunny
stands watch inside the door. Cutter will stand on the sidewalk and
keep watch there. Rahmi is out back in the alley by the backdoor. I'll
be in the van with the motor running. I only get out if something goes
sideways and Cutter needs backup.

Grissom's sister has even provided the code to shut off the entrance alarm. She only had the code for the front door, but this gives us a leg up. If Grissom's sister fucks like she thieves, she must be a real firecracker.

As the three guys prepare to go inside, Cracker Jack says, "Make sure you guys put on your masks and gloves."

"I hate these fuckin' ski masks," Cunny says. "They make me feel like a stickup kid." Cutter laughs. "You are a fuckin' stickup kid."

Everyone chuckles nervously.

"We've got no choice," Cracker Jack says. "They've got cameras all around here. Especially this rich prick Bill White. Rich people love cameras. They make 'em feel all warm and safe."

"It's our job to show him otherwise," I say.

Cutter says, "Fucking Rahmi left his gloves in here."

"Stupid fuck," mutters Cunny.

"Like I always say, 'never trust a sand nigger'," Cutter says.

Cracker Jack says, "That's what they say about spics like you."

"Well, it ain't what your mother says."

Everyone laughs.

"You guys hurry up in there," Cutter says. "I'm gonna look obvious standing out here on the sidewalk with a ski mask on."

The three of them get out. Cracker Jack and Cunny stand outside the entrance to the office for a moment. Cracker Jack jimmies the door, disables the alarm, and they go inside. We're off to the races. I switch on the radio and scan through the stations as I watch Cutter standing up the street, just beyond the campaign office, smoking a cigarette. He looks nervous. There's no one else on the street. I scan through the stations, moving past country channel after country channel. I finally land on a classic rock station playing "Free Bird". As I watch Cutter, I tap my fingers on the steering wheel. I'm nervous, but this is my favorite part. It's like riding a roller coaster or watching a scary movie; it's about the adrenaline.

I look out the driver-side window for about thirty seconds. When I look back at Cutter, I see him talking to a couple. Cutter is still wearing the black ski mask. Then, all of a sudden, I see Cutter pull out his pistol with his gloved hand and whip the man unconscious. The woman screams. At least it looks like she screams, but I can't actually hear it because the windows are up and Foghat is playing. Now Cutter is chasing her. My heart is racing. "Goddammit, Cutter," I say aloud. Cutter tackles her on the sidewalk. I look up ahead at the bar, but thankfully no one is outside. At almost the exact same time Cutter tackles the girl, Cracker Jack and Cunny emerge from the office. Cracker Jack is carrying a trash sack full of money. Cracker Jack and Cunny stand there watching Cutter as he pistol-whips the girl into submission. Cracker Jack says something to Cutter, and within seconds the three of them are hauling ass back to the van.

They open the doors and hop in. "Slow Ride" is still playing. All the doors shut, and they peel off their masks.

"Jesus fuck, Cutter," Cracker Jack says.

"*What?*" Cutter says. "It couldn't be helped."

"I thought for sure we were gonna get caught," Cunny says.

"How much money did we get?" Cutter asks.

"I don't know, but it's a lot," Cracker Jack says.

"We did good," Cutter says.

"I don't know what the fuck you're talking about," Cracker Jack says. "You didn't do good, Cutter. You fucked us up."

Cutter is indignant. "I didn't fuck up."

"Yes, you did," Cracker Jack says. "You fucked us up."

"No, I didn't."

The Stones come on singing "Honky-Tonk Woman", and Cunny perks up. "Could you turn up the radio?"

"Fuck the radio," Cracker Jack growls. "Turn it off."

I switch off the radio. We drive around to the alley. Rahmi is standing beside the backdoor, smoking. He sees us and drops his cigarette. He climbs into the van.

"How many cigarettes did you smoke?" Cracker Jack asks.

"I dunno," Rahmi says. "Three, maybe four."

"You ain't got no gloves on. Get out and pick up the butts. If they find 'em, they can get prints off of 'em."

"I doubt they will."

Cracker Jack gives him a look that's as hard as steel. "We can't take that chance, moron. Now get out and pick 'em up."

Rahmi shrugs and gets out, still wearing his mask, and starts picking up butts.

"Fucker shoulda saw this coming," Cutter says. "He's a fortune teller. He's supposed to be psychic."

TWENTY-THREE

"Let's put some room between us and that office," Cracker Jack says.

"We gotta dump this van too," Rahmi says.

I already know these things, but I don't say anything. The Who is on the radio now and I've got my foot pressed down on the gas pedal, getting us the fuck out of Dodge. We're on our way out of the city when I pass a cop in the other lane. I keep my eyes on him and see him flip a U. His blue flashers come on. I'm only going a couple of miles over the speed limit, so I'm not sure why he's following us. It might be something, might be nothing, but it doesn't matter since we're in a stolen vehicle.

"Jesus," I say.

"What?" asks Cutter, who hasn't seen the cop.

Cracker Jack sees him, though. "I'll shoot that motherfucker if I gotta."

I maintain my speed, watching the cop in my rearview. "What should I do?"

"You got no choice," Cracker Jack says. "You gotta pull over."

I take the Lord's name in vain for the second time in thirty seconds. I pull over. The cop pulls up behind me. He's sitting there, calling in our tags. He's going to know the vehicle is stolen in about a minute.

"This is some shit," Cunny remarks.

"I'll take care of this," Cracker Jack says.

"No," I say firmly. "I've got this."

Before the cop can get out, I shift into reverse and stomp the gas, backing hard into the front of the cop car. I want to make sure his airbag goes off, trapping him, so I pull forward a little bit further this time and then drop the van into reverse, slamming into the cop car even harder this time.

"*Holy fuck!*" Rahmi says.

Cutter almost falls on the floor.

"*Get us outta here!*" Cracker Jack roars.

I stomp the gas and the Odyssey lurches forward, peeling out.

"We gotta lose this van ASAP," Cutter says.

"No shit," I say.

These fuckers are all saying obvious shit I already know, irritating me. I hook a right at the next corner and then drive a couple blocks, going way too fast. Every time we hit a bump everyone bounces up out of their seats. I take a sharp left. I drive another two blocks and then I take a right. I stop the van on the side of the street in a dark residential area and shut off the lights.

"What are we doing here?" Cunny asks.

"We're about to haul ass," Cracker Jack says. "Just shut your mouth and skedaddle."

We all hop out, shut the doors, and take off running down the dark street. Cracker Jack and I are side by side, leading the way.

"Let's take this alley," I say. I cut to the right, not even looking to see if Cracker Jack is coming. Fuck this, I'm not getting arrested. They can do whatever they want, but I'm not going to prison. I hear sirens in the distance. My heart is pounding, and it feels like it's in my throat.

"Where we going?" a winded Cutter asks behind me.

No one answers. We just keep running. I hook a left at the next corner, and everyone follows. I turn to Cracker Jack, who's behind to my right. "We've gotta get outta sight." He grunts his approval. I point towards a house with no lights on. I sprint up the steps onto the porch and bang on the door. I wait for about thirty seconds. I'm just about to bang again when it opens. An old black man in a robe looks out, squinting. "Who the hell are you?" Before I can answer, Cracker Jack's got his Glock up in the man's face, saying, "Shut your mouth and let us in." The man nods and moves out of the way. We all go inside the dark house.

"Somebody turn the lights on," Rahmi says.

"No," Cracker Jack says. "Leave 'em off. It'll be obvious if this is the only house on the block that's lit up like Christmas." He looks at the old man. "Is there anyone else in the house with you?"

"No," the man says. "Just me and you stupid hillbilly motherfuckers."

"You better watch your mouth."

"I didn't serve two tours in Nam to come home and take shit like this off a bunch of white trash sons of whores like you."

"Shut your face or I'll put a bullet through it."

Cunny asks, "What do we do now?"

"We wait," says Cracker Jack.

"How long you plannin' on waitin' here?" the old man asks.

"Until tomorrow morning around eight or nine," Cracker Jack says. "Then, if the coast is clear, we're gonna steal your car and get the hell outta here."

There's a long pause before the old man asks, "What are you gonna do with me?"

"That's up to you," Cracker Jack says. "If you do the right thing, we'll do the right thing."

"You'll let me live?"

"Sure we will."

TWENTY-FOUR

CRACKER JACK CALLED Sammy before we left Jeff City, and Sammy sent Sonny Cafferty to pick us up in Bagnell, where we dumped the dead man's Cutlass. Sonny arrives in a burgundy Toyota Sienna. Sonny is a chain-smoking old timer who's pushing sixty. The guy's spent more time in the joint than I've been alive. I don't care for him because he's dumber than a box of hammers, and he always smells like a combination of onions, feet, and farts, all rolled up in one fat, grubby package. When we climb into the Sienna, the van is filled with smoke and Sonny is puffing away on what's probably his fortieth cigarette of the morning. Cunny Jaymes and Sonny are old pals, so Cunny sits up front next to Sonny. *Sonny & Cunny*, I think. Sounds like a TV show. A really shit one I would never watch, because fuck these clowns.

On the way to Funland, Sonny and Cunny attempt to trade stories of prison life, but Cutter ends up dominating the conversation the same bullshit sex stories we've all heard a hundred times. This time he tells us two of his favorites. The first is about a time he fucked a girl without a condom. He didn't have one, so he wrapped a bread sack around his dick, using a rubber band to hold it on. Then he says,

"Another time I was looking for a bread bag but couldn't find one, so I had to use aluminum foil. I just crinkled it up around my dick real tight. There were jagged little edges around the sides, but I used it anyway. It cut her up real bad. When I pulled it out, it was drenched in blood."

The second story Cutter shares is one about him screwing a chick who had a one-year-old baby. Cutter says the baby was asleep in a playpen beside the bed. "We were fuckin' and I glance over and see that the baby is awake now," he says. "And the baby is just sitting there staring at me with these sad eyes like, 'Why you fuckin' my mama?' It drove me nuts, but I didn't wanna stop bangin' her, so I took a blanket and threw it on top of the baby's head so he couldn't watch us no more. The baby started crying, but we didn't stop. I just kept right on, plowing like Farmer Dave." Cutter stops and smirks. "Funny thing, but with that baby crying, I had the hardest orgasm I've ever had." He pauses. "I don't know what that says about me."

Cracker Jack looks at him. "It says you're a fuckin' degenerate is what it says."

TWENTY-FIVE

THERE ENDED up being half a million in cash. Cracker Jack also found a bag full of uncut diamonds in the safe, as well as some papers that turned out to be German bearer bonds. In all, we ended up scoring just under three million dollars. Needless to say, we were all extremely happy, and everyone made out like a bandit. But then we are bandits, but who's keeping score?

A few days later, Sammy throws us a small party at the Dirty Bird. The Dirty Bird is a rundown hillbilly beer joint he owns that's located a few miles East of Branson. Everyone from the robbery is here except Cunny Jaymes. There's also Sammy, his niece Bella, who of course sucks him off right there in front of us, Lou the bartender, and Virgil Jessup, the Taney County Sheriff. I don't much like cops, but Virgil is so corrupt I don't even consider him one. To say he's on the take would be as big an understatement as saying Jimi Hendrix once came in contact with a guitar. Virgil is around all the time and doesn't even try to hide the fact that he's as big a criminal as the rest of us.

Tammy Wynette is on the jukebox singing "Stand By Your Man." All of us are drunk. Not just shitfaced, but thirty-two sheets to the wind. We're so fucked up that Cracker Jack, Cutter, and Virgil are playing Russian Roulette with Sammy's .38 Chiefs Special. Sammy, Rahmi, and me all say fuck that, we don't wanna play. But we watch because it's a train wreck we can't tear our eyes away from.

Cracker Jack puts the .38 to his temple nonchalantly and pulls the trigger. *Click!* Everyone chuckles and the conversation continues. Cutter is telling one of his stories when Virgil pipes up. "You still fuckin' around with that little dick-sucker works over at The Booby Trap?" Everyone except for Virgil and Lou the bartender knows how much Cutter cares about Kammie, so we all just watch, waiting to see what Cutter is gonna do.

Cutter stares at Virgil. "Why don't you mind your own business, you dick-ass motherfucker?"

Everyone laughs an uneasy laugh and Virgil spins the cylinder before putting the pistol to his temple. "I didn't mean nothing," he says. He takes another swig of his whiskey and pulls the trigger. *Click!* He smirks and his eyes get big. He's trying to pretend he wasn't frightened, but fucking Ray Charles can see he was. And this is saying something because Ray Charles is blind and dead. But trust me, Ray Charles could fucking see it.

Virgil passes the .38 to Cutter. Cutter smiles a big maniacal smile and holds the .38 to his temple, squeezing the trigger like it's nothing. *Click!*

There's a titter of laughter.

"*I'm too evil to die!*" he roars.

More laughter.

Cutter spins the cylinder and passes the .38 to Cracker Jack. Cracker Jack takes a swig of whiskey, puts the pistol to his head, nonchalant as you please, and squeezes the trigger. *Click!*

"I'm starting to think the fucking pistol isn't loaded," Virgil says as he takes the .38. He's sweating like a Tijuana hooker on two-for-one night. He takes another drink. His hand is shaking. Not much, but it's visible. He raises the pistol to his temple. "Imagine if I shot myself in the head right after saying I didn't think it was loaded," he says. "I'd look like a real dumb motherfucker."

"You are a dumb motherfucker," Cutter says, trying to sound like he's joking. I know Cutter well enough to know he isn't.

Virgil sighs and does a half-shrug. He closes his eyes and squeezes the trigger. *Click!* Virgil relaxes a little and laughs uneasily. He looks at Cutter and says, "I may be a dumb motherfucker, but at least I'm smart enough not to fall in love with a bitch who's probably sucked off everyone at the table."

Cutter's staring at him like he's just been slapped. I try to lighten the mood and say, "Not me. I never fucked her." I'm lying of course, but no one here knows that. Then Bella, sitting naked on Sammy's lap, says, "Me neither!"

Everyone laughs, but my eyes are on Cutter. Virgil hands him the .38. I'm worried Cutter is gonna shoot Virgil, but he doesn't. He spins the cylinder before raising the pistol to his temple. He grins a dumb grin. "This fucker here," he says, staring at Virgil. I figure Cutter's gonna let it slide tonight since we're here with Sammy, but I know he won't let it slide forever. Cutter isn't the forgiving type. He's the kind of guy who, if you pissed him off and he died, would come back as a ghost and haunt your ass in the afterlife.

Cutter takes a drink. He takes a breath and says, "Here goes nothing." He looks like he's gonna pull the trigger, but instead he swivels the pistol around and aims it at Virgil, sticking it right in the fucking guy's face. He squeezes the trigger. *Click!*

Virgil looks like he's about to shit himself. He looks at Sammy for help. *"Please no!"*

Sammy shrugs, smoking his cigar. "You insulted his woman."

Virgil looks at Cutter, who's still got the .38 in his face. "I didn't mean nothing."

Cutter grins. "Yeah, you did. You meant it all. All of it, you doggie-knobbin' piece of shit." He squeezes the trigger. *Click!* Virgil jumps out of fear. "What can I do, Cutter? You name it, I'll do it."

"You shouldn't have insulted her," I say.

"He's right," Cracker Jack says.

"Please," Virgil says with teary eyes.

Cutter squeezes the trigger again. *Click!* Cutter makes a confused face and holds up the pistol, examining it. Then he aims it at Virgil's face and squeezes four times in quick succession. *Click! Click! Click! Click!*

"Motherfucker!" Cutter says. "It ain't loaded."

Virgil looks relieved.

Rahmi looks at him. "You got lucky, pal."

Sammy laughs. "I was fucking with you guys. I took all the bullets out."

Virgil is smiling when Cutter goes over the table, smacking him across the face with the pistol. Cutter climbs on top of him and just keeps smashing Virgil's face, over and over. Virgil's face is losing definition as his skull breaks apart. *"I'll teach you to disrespect my Kammie, you rat fuck!"* No one tries to stop or calm Cutter, and Cutter pounds away on Virgil well past the poor bastard's demise. When Cutter is finally finished, he stands erect, looking at all of us with a tired look. There's blood all over his face and his once Beastie Boys shirt is now drenched in blood. He sits back down and finishes his drink. He looks over at Lou the bartender. "I'm sorry, Lou. I really am."

"For what?" Lou asks. Cutter looks at Sammy, who nods permission. Cutter comes up with his own .45 now and fires a slug through the bartender's eye, killing the only potential witness.

Cutter look around the table and moves his arm in a circular motion like a windmill, saying, "I hurt my arm when I went across the table. I think it's my rotator cuff."

"I guess you ain't gonna pitch for the Yankees now," I joke.

"Fuck the Yankees!" Cutter says.

Sammy says, "Your arm better heal real quick, because you got a fuckin' mess to clean up."

TWENTY-SIX

YEAR THREE

NOT MUCH HAS CHANGED in the seven months Grace and I have been together, except that Bill White has become the governor. Despite that, no one has ever come sniffing around for the money, which is crazy because I was sure they would. Cutter and Kammie are still together, and they've gotten really close, but he hasn't popped the question yet. Grace and I have grown close too. Tonight, it's Kammie's birthday and the four of us are double-dating at the Tuscaloosa Grill, a bar in Branson that Sammy doesn't own.

Grace and Kammie get along well. They're not best friends like Cutter and me, but they're cool with each other. The four of us have been double-dating for a while now. At first, I felt bad for leaving Cracker Jack out, but Cracker Jack just laughed when I mentioned it. "Don't feel bad," he said. "I don't have a woman because I don't want a woman. I get enough pussy bangin' the whores at the club, and there's no way in hell I'm taking any of them out in public." We both laughed, but then we both remembered Cutter being with Kammie. Neither of us mentioned it.

We're at the table and a Post Malone song comes on. I don't know which one because all that shit sounds the same to me. I'm sitting here smoking a cigarette and nodding my head to the rhythm, listening to the girls discussing Drake songs. "Drake is a pretty good-looking guy," Kammie says. "I would totally fuck him." I'm looking at Cutter the moment Kammie says this, and his demeanor changes instantly. His face goes slack and he goes from happy-go-lucky club guy to pissed-off-looking jealous guy in a matter of seconds. "What did you say?" he asks. I look at Grace and we both roll our eyes. "Don't you think it's disrespectful to talk about wantin' to fuck another dude while I'm sitting here?"

"What do you care?" she asks. "Were you under the mistaken impression I was a virgin?"

She laughs. Grace and I both want to laugh, but we hold it in.

"I'm just saying I don't appreciate that shit."

Kammie leans over and runs her hand up his inner thigh. "I'll make it up to you later, baby."

And just like that, Cutter's demeanor changes. "Sure, okay," he says. "That works for me."

She smiles. "Somehow I thought you'd say that."

He looks around the table. "I'm gonna get a drink. Anybody else need anything?"

"I'll have a beer," I say. He nods and says, "Sure thing."

Grace looks at me. "I gotta pee. I'll be back in a jiffy."

I smile. "I'll be right here waiting."

She stands and smiles. "Good." Then she looks at Kammie and jokes, "Can I trust the two of you?"

"Of course," we say in unison.

No sooner than Grace is gone, Kammie looks at me and says, "So when are we gonna fuck?"

My eyes open wide and I do a double take. "Come again?"

"I'm serious," she says grinning.

"We already fucked," I say, watching Cutter up at the bar, trying to get the bartender's attention.

"No," she says. "That was work. That don't count."

I give her a serious look. "Cutter's my best friend and he loves you. No way in hell I'm doing that."

Her devilish grin widens, and I feel her foot rubbing my shin. "What he don't know won't hurt him. Besides, I'm not really a one guy kinda girl."

I lean in, still watching Cutter, who's looking the other way. "I get that, Kammie, but I can't. It's nothing against you. You're a pretty girl..."

"Pretty?" she blinks.

"I just can't," I say. "And I've got Grace."

"Do you love her?"

"I do," I say. "I love both of them."

She rolls her eyes. "You're no fun."

"What can I say?" I ask, trying to lighten things.

She locks her eyes on mine. "You can say you'll fuck the taste out of my mouth. That's what you can say. You can say you'll fuck me so hard my eyes'll pop out of my head. You can say you'll use me like a dirty little whore. Come on, Billy. You know you wanna."

She's right, I do. But I've got a good thing with Grace and I'm not messing that up for anyone, let alone a skank like Kammie. Besides, I love Cutter like a brother, and I would never do that shit. We watch out for each other. Is my dick hard right now? You bet it is, but I'm gonna go home, fuck Grace, and call it a night.

Grace is the first one back to the table. "Cutter's still gone? It's taking a while."

"It is," I say, looking up at Cutter, who's bringing a whole tray of beers back. When he reaches the table, he's all smiles. "Did I miss anything?"

"Nothing important," Kammie says. "Nothing except for Billy trying to steal me away."

Cutter looks at me and I laugh. Kammie says, "He said he was gonna steal me away, but I told him hell no, I got a man."

Grace grabs my arm, playing along. "Billy's mine."

"We'll share him," Kammie jokes.

Cutter laughs and shakes his head. "These women of ours are no good."

If you only knew, Cutter. If you only knew.

TWENTY-SEVEN

THE FOUR OF us close the bar. It's five till two. We're all staggering to our cars and Kammie looks up at sky. "The stars are really pretty tonight."

Now we're all standing in the parking lot staring up at the sky. Grace points. "There's the big dipper."

Kammie says, "I used to know all the constellations."

I never knew any of them. I hear people talk about the big dipper and the little dipper, but I don't know shit about any dippers. I never had much interest in that. When I was a kid, I had a friend who wanted to be in NASA, but I was more interested in playing ball or being a guitar player.

"You wanna see the prettiest star of all?" Cutter asks.

We're all staring at those stupid stars, waiting for Cutter to finish. Kammie says, "What?"

"Look," he says. We all turn to see him holding an open ring box. I can't see it very well from where I'm standing, but I know what it is.

"Is that what I think it is?" Kammie asks.

Cutter grins. "That depends on what you think it is."

Kammie starts to cry. "Oh, Cutter!" She throws her arms around him. He grins at me as she hugs him. I look at Grace, who's looking at me expectantly.

I hold the palms of my hands out in front of me. "I'm sorry. I don't have any rings."

Grace grins, but I can see on her face that she wants a ring too. Rings are like roses and babies; if one girl gets them, they all want them.

TWENTY-EIGHT

I HELD out for another month, but I really wanted to ask Grace to marry me. When I finally decided to buy a ring, I knew I had to get one as nice as the one Cutter bought. But I also didn't want to show him up or screw up Kammie's big moment, so I was careful. I ended up buying a nice used ring from Kirby Carnahan's pawn shop on Commercial Street. Cutter and I know Kirby fairly well since he's one of the shop owners who buy Reverend Sammy's insurance; as long as they pay a monthly fee, their stores won't burn down. At least not by our hand. If their store does get torched or robbed, the store owners have Sammy's help tracking down the no-good bastards.

I bought a 14-karat white gold ring. Kirby called it a "round and baguette cut," but I don't know what that means. All I know was that the fucking thing ended up costing me a couple grand. Kirby said it would have cost another grand if I'd purchased it new, so at least there's that.

I tried like hell to figure out some grand way to propose. The sweet stuff doesn't mean all that much to me, but I know women are into that kind of shit. I never did come up with anything, but I know whatever I do is gonna be better than Cutter's drunken proposal outside the bar. I've been carrying the ring box in my jeans pocket, waiting for the right moment.

Tonight, we're at the drive-in in Aurora, which is about an hour from Funland. I don't know why, but I've always loved the drive-in although I don't go very often. I'm not a big movie buff like Grace is, but I do like the occasional flick. Tonight's double bill is a Burt Reynolds double feature—*Smokey and the Bandit* and *White Lightning*. On one of our first dates, we watched *Deliverance* together at Grace's place and we talked about our mutual appreciation of Burt Reynolds. She thought he was "super sexy", but I just thought he was a cool motherfucker. Not quite as cool as Charles Bronson, mind you, but pretty high up on the coolness totem pole. Grace said she would have loved to have fucked Burt Reynolds. To this I'd said, "He was an old-ass man!" This made her laugh and she said, "No, not when he was old. When he was young." I asked her how young—*Deliverance* young or *Smokey and the Bandit* young? She said either way would have been fine by her. Then she looked at me and asked, "Would you fuck Burt Reynolds?" I laughed. "What?! No way!" Then she had pressed and asked if I was forced to fuck a guy, would I fuck Burt Reynolds. I told her dick wasn't on the menu for me and that I'd have to pass. She kept pressing and pressing, wanting me to say I'd fuck Burt Reynolds, but I kept saying no. But truth be told, maybe I would have. But you know, only if I absolutely *had* to fuck a dude. But I can't imagine any scenario like that occurring, and also Burt is dead and in the ground, so none of it matters anyway.

We're in my new Blazer—the one I bought after we robbed Bill White. We're midway through *White Lightning* when I feel Grace's hand on my cock. I turn and look at her. I might have given her a fucked-up look because she immediately says, "What? You don't like that?" I'm tempted to tell her that I really wanna watch the movie because it's a pretty fucking badass movie, but I reconsider. If I say no, my dick will never forgive me. It's not like we haven't done the bone dance before, but right now my dick is hard enough to cut diamonds. I look into her eyes and lean in. We start to kiss, and soon my hands are unfastening her bra. Before either of us knows what's happening, we're both stripping off our clothes. *White Lightning* isn't a particularly sexy film, but before long we've got the passenger seat reclined and I'm riding Grace like a thoroughbred at Preakness. I'm grinding on top of her, and it occurs to me that we're only a few feet away from other cars. Cars that might have kids in them but fuck it; I figure I'll give them a show they'll never forget.

Grace comes hard and fast. Then she comes a second time and moans the sexiest, most dick-stiffening moan I've ever heard. She looks into my eyes as I'm escalating towards ejaculation. "Do you love me, Billy?" "Yes," I say. "Are you sure?" "Oh yeah."

"How much?" I'm on the precipice of an orgasm when I look into her eyes and say, *"I wanna marry you, Gracie Girl!"* She's trembling. "Really?" *"Yes!"* I say. *"Yes! Yes! Yes!"* And I cum harder than any man has ever cum.

After that, we just hold each other. I think about the cars around us but don't care. I pull back to look into her eyes again. Grace asks, "Did you mean that?"

"That I wanted to marry you?"

"Yeah."

"I did."

She coos, which is a sound I've never heard a woman make.

"Are you going to ask me?"

"If I ask, what will you say?"

Her eyes catch the light and glimmer. "Ask me and find out."

I climb off her and lift myself over her Diet Coke and into my seat. My thigh hurts like hell because the seat belt fastener has been poking me the whole time. I reach down to the floor for my jeans. I grab them and retrieve the ring box from the pocket and present it to her.

We're both still naked when she opens it. She looks at me and I say, "Grace, will you marry me?"

Tears suddenly emerge from her eyes. "Of course I will, Billy." She looks back at the ring. "This is the most romantic thing ever."

Before we can put our clothes on, there's a knock on the driver's side window. I turn and look to see a fat balding man in a bowling shirt staring at me. He motions for me to roll down the window, so I do. He says, "You can't do whatever it is you're doin' here."

"Who the fuck are you?" I ask.

"I'm the manager. Who do you think I am?"

I stare at him, trying to decide what to say. Then it comes to me. I reach down and pop the lid off the Diet Coke. Then I turn and hurl the drink at him, and he jumps like I've thrown a fireball.

"You better get the fuck outta here before I bust out your goddamn teeth," I say. He looks at me with a scared expression and leaves. I turn and look at Grace. "We better get outta here," she says.

"I love you, Gracie Girl."

"I love you too."

If this isn't romance, I don't know what the hell is.

TWENTY-NINE

IT's our wedding day and I'm nervous. Cutter and Kammie convinced me to make it a double-wedding, which didn't go over too well with Grace. I agreed to it without speaking to Grace, so she was angry. Turns out she doesn't like Kammie nearly as much as I thought she did. Sometimes I think about how she'd hit the roof if she knew about Kammie coming onto me. And she would *really* hit the roof if she knew about the night I came *into* Kammie. I'm just hoping like hell Kammie never mentions it to Cutter, because if she does it's gonna be a problem.

We're all four standing at the front of the First Redeemer Church. I'm staring into Grace's eyes, and Cutter and Kammie are looking at each other a few feet behind me. Reverend Sammy is officiating, and he's wearing a green and white track suit with a gold chain and orange crocs. The whole thing is strange. I don't know the Bible real well, but I believe a lot of what he's saying is just shit he's making up because he knows no one else here has read it. But again, I don't know much about the Bible, so I can't be sure. I'm listening to him talk about the sanctity of marriage, and I suddenly recognize several of the lines he's saying as lyrics from "When a Man Loves a

Woman." He's saying it's from the Bible, which I'm pretty sure is horseshit. Then he goes back to saying some more stuff about love and marriage, which sounds like it probably did come out from the Bible. But then he starts telling a story about soldiers coming home after World War One and finding that their loves had left yellow ribbons tied around the trees. He says this is a story from the old testament, but that sounds like a lie to me. I don't know as a fact, but I'm pretty sure there aren't any stories about World War One in the Bible. I'm not sure when World War One happened, but I've seen pictures of tanks and airplanes, so I'm pretty sure it occurred after the Bible.

Sammy announces that he has a special treat. I have no idea what it is because Sammy told us, "Don't worry about anything. I got it all under control." He introduces a "very special singer" and brings out Bella, dressed in a ridiculously skimpy "fuck me" outfit. Sure, I've banged her in the ass a few times, but I've never really given her any thought. But seeing her in that tiny black outfit, I've got to admit I've got wood.

She points at an old lady sitting off to the side at a soundboard and the lady hits some buttons. "I Want It That Way" comes on, and Bella starts dancing like the Backstreet Boys, only if the Backstreet Boys had Parkinson's. She's clapping wildly and breathing heavily into the mic. Then she warbles the most horrible version of this already horrible song. And it's official; my hard-on is gone with the wind. It's incredibly awkward standing here in front of the church, staring into Grace's eyes while Bella attempts to sing. Grace and I are trying our best not to giggle, but looking into each other's eyes just makes us want to giggle more so we have to stare at each other's foreheads.

The song finally wraps up, and everyone looks around awkwardly like they're not sure if they should clap. Sammy steps up and slaps Bella on her ass and she giggles. "Let's it hear it for my niece, Bella," he says. "Hell of a singer, that girl. I tell you, she's good at just about everything." Sammy chuckles to himself. "Okay," he says. "This is the moment you've all been waiting for." I look at Grace and we both smile, ready to be married.

"Do you, Kammie, promise to honor and cherish your husband, in sickness and in health?" Sammy says.

"I do," I hear Kammie say.

Sammy says, "Do you promise you'll stay with him, even if he gets the clap or some other type of STD?"

There's a pause. Then I hear Kammie say, *"His ass better not get an STD!"*

The whole church erupts into laughter, and I hear Cutter saying, "Come on, Sammy."

More laughter.

"Okay, Kammie, do you take Cutter to be—"

"Uh, Manny," Cutter says.

"Oh yeah," Sammy says. "Manny. Okay, do you promise to take this little spic fuck to be your lawfully wedded husband through sickness, health, poverty, STDs, and whatever else?"

Kammie says, "I guess that about covers it, huh?"

Another titter of laughter.

"Sure," Kammie says. "I take him."

"Ahhhh, okay," Sammy says. "How about you Cutter? Do you take Kammie to be your faithfully devoted and loving wife?"

"Manny," Cutter reminds him.

"Okay, okay, yeah."

"It's okay," Cutter says. "I take her."

Sammy says, "Okay, cool." Then he turns towards us. Grace and I exchange a look about how weird this wedding has turned.

"I need you guys to look at me," Sammy says.

Still holding hands, we turn toward him.

Sammy grins and then winks. He clears his throat. "Do you, Grace, promise to honor and love, and maybe even give some blowjobs to your man Bill here, through sickness and disease and cancer and…" Sammy pauses and smirks, looking at Grace. "This fucker smokes like a damn chimney. I think we all know he's gonna get cancer."

Everyone in the room laughs. I don't think me getting cancer is particularly funny, but whatever.

"Do you promise to honor and cherish and just basically stay with him, through thick and thin, no matter what?"

She nods. "I do."

"Good," Sammy says. "Okay, Bill, you're up to bat. Do you Billy Hanson take this fine-ass woman here to be your lawfully wedded wife? Do you promise to stay with her and take care of her and do whatever the hell needs to be done like a good husband, no matter what, until the end of time and maybe even longer?"

I look into Grace's eyes. "I do."

"Hallelujah," Sammy says. "Praise God, God is good. Then by the powers given to me by the state of Missouri, this here church, and Jesus hisself up in heaven, I now declare you all man... okay, okay... *men* and *wives*. Fellas, you can now kiss your fine-ass brides."

THIRTY

THE RECEPTION IS in the church, in the same fellowship hall where we met Grissom and Marshall. Sammy organized it, which is good and bad. It's good because allowing him to do this makes Cutter and me tighter with him and spares us from spending money and time setting it up, but also bad because the old man has questionable tastes.

The music is a band called BanJovi, which is a Bon Jovi cover band that plays everything with a banjo. I thought Bon Jovi was trash before, but man, I've got a new respect for them now because their songs sound so much worse with a fucking banjo. I'm standing beside Grace, sipping punch that's been spiked by fifty different people with at least as many alcohols, and Sammy is pointing at the band and telling me how great they are. They're singing "It's My Life" and he's in my face, so close I can smell his nasty breath.

"They're good, huh?" he says. "You know, these guys were ranked as the third best Bon Jovi cover band in Missouri."

"Huh," I say noncommittally.

"You won't believe this, but I met Jon Bon Jovi at an orgy in Tallahassee back in '93."

He's right, I don't believe it.

"You shoulda seen the schlong on that guy!"

Grace looks at him. "It was big?"

"Big as a jig."

I turn to Sammy. "You lived in Florida?"

He nods. "For a bit."

"Whereabouts?"

"All over, I guess. But that's me—all over the place."

"I lived in Shreveport, and then later on aways a way on the Red River."

He pats me on my back. "All the best people come from Florida."

Or the worst, I think.

I look at Grace and smile. Sammy is watching Banjovi destroy a song that wasn't good to begin with, and he's clapping along and tapping one of his crocs. He turns to Grace. "Do you like Bon Jovi, sweetheart?"

She's a deer caught in headlights. "Is this a test?"

"No, no," he says. "I was just wondering."

"They're pretty good, I guess."

This seems to be enough for him and he goes back to watching the band. Then he turns to me. "I got a DJ coming up after this. You'll love him. He's a one-legged dwarf!" He says it in a way that suggests the DJ might be better because of this.

We mill around and talk and cut the cake and all that, and then finally, the DJ shows up with another guy—a taller guy with both legs —and they get the equipment set up. Eventually the band leaves, and the DJ starts playing pop songs. A lot of people dance. By now everyone's drunk, so it's sort of fun to watch them staggering around. I don't dance, partially because I don't know how and partially because I think dancing is for women and fags. Cutter and me stand off to the side and watch everyone dance, our wives included.

"Where's Cracker Jack?" I ask.

Cutter looks around. "I guess he skipped out on us."

"Rat bastard."

Cutter looks at me and grins. "He's definitely a rat bastard."

I ask him how he likes being married.

"I'm not sure yet," he says. "Ask me tomorrow."

I ask him if he plans to be monogamous.

"What's that?" he asks.

"Are you gonna be faithful?"

He looks at me deathly serious. "Of course. I'm gonna be faithful to Kammie forever." He pauses. "You can be faithful and still bang other broads, you know."

"You gonna have an open relationship where you both sleep with other people?"

He looks at me angrily. "Fuck no! She better never cheat. What I'm saying is, I can love and respect her—all the stuff Sammy said—and still fuck other girls."

"And get head," I offer, just to see what he'll say.

"Right! Head don't count!"

"And eatin' ain't cheatin'," I say.

So, just as I figured, Cutter's gonna keep doing what he's been doing, screwing every woman in sight. But I'm not saying a word. He's a big boy. If he wants to do that shit, let him.

We're watching our drunk wives dancing to a Tupac song when Kammie accidentally steps on the train of Grace's dress, causing her to stumble and fall.

"Oh shit!" Cutter and I say in unison.

Grace stands up and charges Kammie, belting her in the mouth, and Kammie goes down hard. Cutter and I both move forward, and the girls are on the floor now, rolling around punching each other. We separate them.

"Well," I say, "I guess it's time to go home."

Neither Cutter nor me are angry. He looks at me and shrugs with his shoulders as he escorts Kammie out.

When we we're outside and in the car, Kammie says, "Did you see how I punched that bitch?"

"I did," I say proudly. "You punched the hell outta that bitch."

THIRTY-ONE

AFTER THE BILL WHITE JOB, Sammy allowed Cutter and me to get houses outside Funland, so we got identical double wides and set them up next to each other down the road. I'm at home and Grace is asleep now, having just won her fight with Kammie. I'm sitting on the couch watching *Rockford Files* when somebody knocks on the door. I get up and grab my Walther PPK like I do anytime someone knocks late at night. I open the door to find Cutter standing there.

"What do you need?" I ask. "It's after midnight."

He's got a weird expression on his face. "I'm gonna need you to come with me for a little while."

"I just got Grace to sleep and I'm tired."

"Cracker Jack's got a surprise for us. He says it's our wedding gift."

"It can't wait until morning?"

"He says it can't wait."

I stare at him for a beat, considering this. "Any idea what it is?"

"Not a fuckin' clue."

"Well, shit. Did he say how long this is gonna take?"

Cutter tilts his head and his mouth twists into a pucker as he shrugs. "He said it might be a while."

"Okay, I gotta write Grace a note. If she wakes up and I'm gone, she's gonna wonder where the hell I am."

"That bitch ain't wakin' up anytime soon," Cutter says. "She's drunker than a welfare wino on the first of the month."

I've got my back to him and I'm writing Grace a note. "Where did you tell Kammie you were going?"

"Are you kidding? She was asleep before we even got home. I had to carry her ass in and put her to bed in her dress."

I step out, closing and locking the door. We walk out to the big F-10 extended cab pickup that Cracker Jack got after the heist. Cutter opens the passenger door and Cracker Jack is behind the wheel, smiling big.

"Billy, my boy," he says. "Wait till you see what I got you!"

Cutter climbs into the back seat. I'm in front.

"You guys want a hint?" Cracker Jack asks.

"Of course we do, ya fuckin' prick!" Cutter says.

Cracker Jack produces a ring box and pushes it towards me.

"What the fuck is this?" I ask.

Cutter says, "We're already married, ya fag."

"Just open it," Cracker Jack says with a mischievous twinkle in his eye.

I open it and find a human finger inside. *"What the fuck?!"*

"Look at it."

There's a ring on the finger. When I look closely, I see that it's got a 'C' on it. I turn to look at Cracker Jack, who's got the biggest goddamn Santa Claus grin on his face.

"This is that cop's finger!" I say.

"Holy shit!" Cutter says.

"Jeremy Caparello," I say.

Cracker Jack smiles wider. "One in the same. One in the fucking same."

"Billy's the one got a problem with this prick," Cutter says, "so how exactly is this a wedding gift for me?"

"Because you like hurting people," Cracker Jack says. "Tell me it ain't so."

Cutter pauses, grinning. "Okay, sure, you got me." He puts his hand on my shoulder. "And for you, Bill, I'll hurt that motherfucker twice as bad!"

"*We'll* hurt him," I correct. "This motherfucker's mine. There's no way on God's green earth he gets hurt and I don't get to do it."

Cracker Jack starts the ignition and puts the truck in drive.

"You'll get your share," Cracker Jack says. "You can hurt him as much as you like."

I look at the finger again, marveling at it.

Cutter asks, "Where the fuck is this cop anyway?"

Without taking his eyes from the road, Cracker Jack says, "He's already out in the woods, waiting for us."

"What the fuck?" I ask.

Cracker Jack turns towards me, still wearing the big smile. "You'll see."

THIRTY-TWO

When we stop on the road, deep in the woods, Cracker Jack is giggling like a schoolgirl. We all get out. "Come on," he says, switching on his flashlight and leading the way. I don't see any lights and I don't hear Jeremy, so I'm curious about what's happening.

Cracker Jack shines the light around. I've got no idea what he's looking for. It's dark. Real dark. Finally, Cracker Jack comes to a spot and says, "Here." He moves the light, and I see a shallow hole.

"What's this?" I ask.

"The fucker's buried there," Cracker Jack says. "In a box, just under the ground."

I gasp. "You already killed him?"

"Calm your tits," Cracker Jack says. "I would never take that from you."

"Then what?"

He's turns towards me. "I made him dig the hole. Then I threw just enough dirt on top to freak him out. I wanted him to think I was burying him alive."

"*Holy shit!*" says Cutter, on the verge of laughter. "You're a sick fuck, you fuckin' sicko!"

"I wanted to torture him, get him prepped for you, so I figured I'd bury him there for an hour or so," Cracker Jack says. "He's gonna be worn out, but his dumb pig ass is alive in there. He's a real asshole."

I say, "I'm well aware."

"Didn't you bring a lantern?" Cutter asks.

Cracker Jack turns and shines his light on one, sitting near the hole. "It's over there. I'll turn it on."

"Is he gonna jump out and try and attack us?" Cutter asks.

"He's handcuffed in there. Behind his back, real, real tight so it hurts, the way the cops like to do it."

Cracker Jack and Cutter both chuckle.

I've got an idea. "He's handcuffed in there?"

"What are you, a fuckin' parrot?" Cracker Jack says. "He's handcuffed."

"Well," I say, "maybe we open it up and I take a piss in his face."

Cutter laughs a hearty laugh.

"Waterboard his ass!" Cracker Jack says. "I like it."

"I got an even better idea," Cutter says. "How about we open the box, and we *all* piss on his face?"

We all laugh.

"We gotta work this out first," Cracker Jack says. "Who's gonna piss on his face first?"

"We're gonna take turns?" I ask.

"What?" Cracker Jack says. "You don't wanna?"

"I figured we'd piss on his face at the same time."

"That's not as good," Cutter says.

We argue about this for a moment, debating the merits of how best to piss on Jeremy's face. We finally decide to take turns, so it takes longer. I agree to this, but only on the grounds that I go first.

Cutter opens the box and Jeremy gasps for air. He's blinking and trying to breathe.

I stand over him. "Hey there, Jeremy, you piece of shit. You remember me? It's Billy Hanson, the guy who stole Grace."

Jeremy's face is dirty, and he looks exhausted. "Fuck you," he manages.

"No," I say. "Fuck you. Look up here, Jeremy. Do you see this?"

I've got my cock out.

"This is the cock that pleasures Grace, you miserable fuck. Take a good look."

"Look close!" Cutter says, laughing.

I let loose and spray a stream of piss into Jeremy's face. He's fighting it, sputtering and spitting, trying to move his face clear of the stream but to no avail. This is a long piss. One that would bubble real good if Jeremy's face was a toilet. All the punch and mixed alcohols from the reception splash in his eyes.

The moment my stream begins to lighten and shorten where it can no longer reach Jeremy's face, Cutter starts spraying.

"Drink it up, you piece of trash," Cutter says. "Drink it, you pig fuck."

When Cutter's piss finally stops, Cutter and I look at Cracker Jack, who's trying to piss but can't.

"What are you waiting for?" Cutter asks.

"Shut up and let me piss," Cracker Jack says. "I got a shy bladder. It don't like to piss in front of people."

Jeremy is watching all this. "You're all gonna pay for this."

"Oh, are we?" I ask. "You gonna make us pay, Jeremy?"

Cutter laughs. Cracker Jack is still trying to piss.

"My police brothers are gonna find you and track you down, one by one, and…"

Cracker Jack's bladder finally relaxes and starts spraying piss. Since Jeremy is in the middle of making his threat, he chokes on it.

THIRTY-THREE

It's immediately apparent that pissing on Jeremy was a bad idea, because now when we punch him or hold him up to punch him, we get piss on our hands and clothes. Maybe the piss will wash away the blood on our hands because there's a lot. Not just Jeremy, but all the dumb fucks who've pissed us off or tried to double-cross Reverend Sammy.

The poor bastard tries to yell a couple times but gets beaten worse each time he does. The first time, he gets punched in the side of the head by Cracker Jack, and it's as hard as anything I've ever seen an MMA fighter throw. The second time Jeremy tries to yell, he's sitting on the ground, on top of his handcuffed hands, and I kick him in the mouth with my steel-toed boot. When I do, Jeremy sprays a handful of teeth.

We finally get tired of beating Jeremy and, Cutter being Cutter, he gouges out one of Jeremy's eyes with a key. It's funny, too, because Cutter is jumping around him screaming, *"That'll serve ya, ya rat fuck! You like that? You love it, don't ya?"* Cutter is always lively, but nothing, and I mean nothing brings him to life like acts of gratuitous violence. Cutter lives for that. For Cracker Jack and me, violence and killing are a part of the job, but for Cutter it *is* the job. His idea of a good time is cutting off a guy's dick, which I've seen him do twice, or stomping on someone's head until it caves in.

When we finally finish with Jeremy—at least the stuff we're gonna do in the woods—he's unconscious. We heft his piss-covered ass into the truck bed. Before we leave, we police the area, making sure we clean up all the teeth Jeremy lost. We pick up eight teeth. Once everything is loaded up, Cutter hops in the back of the truck to babysit Jeremy. Cracker Jack and I get in the cab, and Cracker Jack's behind the wheel again.

Cracker Jack's already made a deal with Mel Kander, who owns the salvage yard near Lampe. Sammy used to take all the bodies there, but Mel complained that there were too many, so Sammy started planting them in the woods.

While we're driving, I hear Jeremy start to scream. I have no idea what Cutter's doing to him, but he's doing something. There's no way he's going to ride with an incapacitated cop and not inflict damage.

When we reach the salvage yard, Cracker Jack drives onto the property and around the garage, straight to the compactor. We've been here enough times we know where it is, and Cracker Jack knows how to work it. Mel has already got an old junker Buick ready and waiting. Jeremy is wide awake and aware of what's happening. Needless to say, he's not thrilled. We cram Cracker Jack's booger-encrusted hankie into his mouth to shut him up, but he's still trying to wiggle and fight.

Cutter comes up with a last-minute idea. He goes to the truck and grabs a can of gas, bringing it over. He opens the car and pours gasoline all over Jeremy, making a point to splash it in his face. Cutter stands in the door of the open car and looks at Cracker Jack, whose finger is on the button. "You ready?" Cutter asks. Cracker Jack says yeah, and Cutter lights his lighter and tosses it in on Jeremy's lap. Suddenly Jeremy is a screaming ball of flames. Cutter shuts the door, giggling. He moves out of the way and Cracker Jack hits the button. We all watch the human fireball Jeremy thrashing around as the sides of the Buick start to close in on him. The rag comes loose from Jeremy's mouth and we hear him scream a high-pitched scream. And then we don't. A moment later, the Buick and Jeremy are just a nice, compact steel box.

"That was fun!" Cutter says.

"I gotta get back to Grace now," I say.

"Too bad it's over," Cracker Jack laments. "I was having fun."

"Me too," Cutter says. "Jeremy was a real prick."

We're all walking back to the truck and I say, "I'm gonna go home and fuck Grace in his honor."

We all laugh.

"He woulda wanted it that way," Cutter says.

I laugh. "Maybe we'll name our baby after Jeremy someday!"

THIRTY-FOUR

YEAR FOUR

WE DON'T NAME the baby Jeremy. We name him Gilbert, after Grace's grandfather who died when she was young. He was her favorite relative and having met the rest of her asshole family I understand why. I wanted to name the baby something more badass, like Ozzy or Thor, but I figured if Grace wants to name the kid Gilbert, then Gilbert it is. When you've got a good thing going, you do whatever it takes to keep it that way. Don't get me wrong, I think Gilbert is a shit name, but it doesn't matter; I'm gonna start calling him Gil before he takes his first step. Then, eventually, he'll just be Gil. It's not the best name ever, but it's a damn sight better than Gilbert.

Grace and I have been married for fourteen months. I was in the birthing room, holding Grace's hand as she delivered the baby. I'm not gonna lie, the childbirth was pretty gross. I know I'm supposed to say it was beautiful and all that, but it was mostly just gross.

Now Grace is asleep in her room and I'm in the waiting room with Cutter and Cracker Jack. I feel bad for Cutter because he and Kammie were gonna have a baby too, but Kammie miscarried. I know it's a sore subject, but he was still the first person to show up at the hospital. The delivery took eight hours, and Cutter stayed the whole time. He might be a lot of things—most of them bad—but he's my best friend.

Cracker Jack gives me a playful slap on the cheek. "What? You're not gonna hand out cigars?"

"I hadn't even thought about it," I say. "I mean, there's only three of us, and none of us like cigars."

This deflates Cracker Jack. "Well, I brought some. They say 'It's a Boy' on 'em."

Now I feel shitty and start backtracking. "Oh, thanks, man. You didn't have to do that. I didn't mean anything by it, but what was I gonna say? I hadn't thought to buy any cigars, so I was just covering my tracks."

Cracker Jack nods. "I know, I know." He reaches into the sack he's holding and pulls out a handful of cigars, wrapped in blue. He hands me a couple and then hands some to Cutter.

"Let's go for a walk," Cracker Jack says. "I got something to tell you guys."

"What?" Cutter asks.

"Like I said, let's walk."

"Goddammit, you can't make it easy, can you?" Cutter says. "If I wanted all this exercise, I'd go to the fuckin' gym!"

We walk outside to the dark parking lot. Cracker Jack looks at me. "Gimme a cigarette, Bill." I swear, Cracker Jack smokes more of my cigs than I do. I pull out the pack and slide one out, handing it over. We both light up. Cutter says, "I'm outta smokes. Can I bum one?"

"I'm sorry," I say. "I've only got one left."

Cutter grins. "It's a good thing I only need one then."

Before I can speak, Cracker Jack tells him, "Smoke the cigar." It's more of a demand than a suggestion. Cutter looks at me and shrugs, unwrapping a cigar.

"So, what's the deal?" I ask.

Cracker Jack squints into the distance. "You ain't gonna believe this."

"Try us," Cutter says.

"How long have I been with Sammy?"

"A long-ass time," I say.

"Right," Cracker Jack says. "A long time."

"So what?" Cutter asks.

"I been doing hits for Sammy for decades."

Cutter and I nod.

"I do good work," Cracker Jack says. "Good, clean work. Nobody can say otherwise."

"One hundred percent true," I say.

"Well, this..." He pauses. "Sammy went and got himself another hitter."

"Sammy did what?!" Cutter says.

"You heard me."

"Why would he do that?" I ask.

"I dunno," Cracker Jack says. "But it's some weirdo from KC. Guy's a fat albino with a blonde mohawk."

"A blonde mohawk?" I say.

Cracker Jack nods. "The guy's a fuckin' whack job. He got a blonde Mr. T mohawk with a mustache and beard. Looks like a cunt."

"That sounds weird," Cutter says.

"Fuck yes, it does," Cracker Jack growls. "Guy's name is Gummy. He's supposed to be big shit in KC."

"And he's takin' your job?" I ask.

"Not exactly," Cracker Jack says. "Sammy says I'll still kill people here and there, but he says it'll free me up to do other things."

"What kinda things?" Cutter asks.

"Fuck if I know," Cracker Jack says.

"You could take up knitting," I say.

"Maybe collect stamps," Cutter adds.

"Learn cooking," I say.

Cracker Jack doesn't laugh. "I don't think Sammy means it as a slight, but it hurts. I've been doing this job for a stretch, and I do good work. But do I get thanked? No. Instead Sammy brings in this... this..."

"Albino," Cutter says.

"Exactly," Cracker Jack says.

"I'm sure it's nothing against you," I say. "Sammy loves you."

He looks me in my eyes to gauge my sincerity. "You think so?"

"I know so."

"Did he say that?"

"Of course he did," I lie. I honestly believe Sammy loves Cracker Jack, but I've never actually heard him say so. But I wanna make the guy feel better. My mama always said it's okay to tell a white lie if it stops somebody from getting hurt. But then my mama said a lot of stupid shit.

Cracker Jack's eyes narrow, like he's a cop trying to read me. "When did he say that?"

"Lots of times."

Now Cutter gets in on it. "Oh yeah," he says. "He's said it lots of times."

Cracker Jack is still staring at us both through narrow eyes. "What did he say specifically?"

Cutter turns and looks at Cracker Jack. "He said he wants to fuck you, okay? He said he wants to grab you by your big fucking head and ram his dick up your ass!"

Cutter and I laugh, but Cracker Jack's still not sure. Then he shrugs and says, "I'm sure you're right." He pats me on my cheek again. "Congrats on the kid, Bill."

THIRTY-FIVE

YEAR FIVE

Sammy's got a new plan regarding the insurance racket. He's stopped charging, having Cutter and me tell business owners that, "due to legal reasons" we can no longer sell them insurance. But we also tell them that if anyone else moves in and starts shaking them down, Sammy would be more than willing to help for a fee. Then Sammy sends in a couple of out-of-town guys to pretend they're freelancers. The guys lean on the businesses harder than we ever did. Then when the business owners are good and afraid, they reach out to us for help. Then we swoop in and save the day for hefty fee, and we do it all without a lifting a finger.

Kirby Carnahan, the guy who owns Branson Pawn calls me. I'm sitting on the couch in my boxers with my feet kicked up, eating Pringles, and watching old music videos. "Hello?"

"Hey, is this Bill?"

I don't recognize the voice. "Who is this?"

"This is Kirby, from the pawn shop. I sold you your wife's ring."

"Oh, yeah," I say. "What's up, Kirby?"

"I got a problem."

"We all got problems."

"You know how you guys quit shaking me down... I mean, how you stopped charging me for insurance?"

"Yeah," I say. "So what?"

"There's some guys coming in and threatening me. They told me I should pay them money. The same kinda deal I was doing with you."

"Yeah?"

"Yeah," Kirby says, "except these cocksuckers want twenty-five percent of everything I make." He pauses. "I'm not a rich guy, Bill."

"I understand."

"These are new guys. I never seen either of them before."

"Where they from?"

"Fuck if I know," Kirby says. "So, I told 'em to take a hike. One of the guys, the fat one, he says, 'Yeah, well, you're gonna regret that.'"

"Okay."

"So, I come in the next day, and my store's been robbed. They didn't take much, but they tore the place up good, like they were tryin' to make a point."

"And did they?"

"What?" Kirby asks.

"Did they make their point?"

Kirby sighs. "Yeah, they did. I don't know what to do."

"So what?" I ask. "Why you callin' me?"

"I didn't know who else to turn to."

"Why didn't you go to the cops?"

He pauses. "You and I both know how that's gonna go down. If I call them, I probably end up lying in a ditch."

"Probably," I say.

"Can you help me? I'm in a bad way here."

Sammy was right. The shop owners are gonna come back *begging* for us to fleece them.

"What were you thinking?" I ask.

"I got an idea," Kirby says. "As weird as it sounds to say this, I felt safer when you guys were shaking me down. I felt like I had protection. At least I knew you."

"We don't do that no more," I say. "My boss has gone straight."

Another pause. "I'm sure he hasn't gone completely straight."

"You don't know my boss."

"Oh, yes I do," Kirby says. "Sammy Gitner, right? No offense, but that guy's as crooked as a cop."

I laugh. "Sammy's done with all that."

"Well," Kirby says, "I was thinking."

"Yeah?"

"I think I got a solution."

"Okay?"

"I wanna talk to Sammy."

"Sammy don't talk to nobody."

"Please, Bill, I need to see him. I got a proposal that will make us all money."

"Yeah?" I say. "What's that?"

"I need to see Sammy. Just tell him I can make him a lot of money."

THIRTY-SIX

WE'RE HAVING a meeting in the backroom at Branson Pawn. It's Cutter, Cracker Jack, Sammy, Kirby, and me. The guy's got us all sitting in lawn chairs like we're schmucks. "Okay, Kirby," Sammy says. "Why'd you bring me down here?"

"I got a business proposition."

"Then let's hear it."

"These guys know me," Kirby says, pointing at me and Cutter. "They know I'm a good guy, that I always paid on time without any problems."

"Kirby was one of our best customers," Cutter says.

Sammy is sitting there with a big fat cigar in his mouth, staring at Kirby. He's not smoking it, on account of the overhead sprinkler system, but he's still got it, unlit, in his mouth. "Okay, so what do you want, Kirby? You tell me, I'll see what I can do."

Kirby stares at him. "I had an idea."

"Stop fucking around," Cutter says.

"What is this genius fuckin' idea you got?" Cracker Jack says.

Kirby doesn't even look at Cracker Jack. His eyes never leave

Sammy's. "I was thinkin' maybe you could come and help me out here."

Sammy leans back, laughing a loud belly-laugh, the front legs of the lawn chair lifting off the ground as he does. "How would I do that?"

"You could be a partner."

"A partner?"

"Yeah," Kirby says. "A silent business partner."

"What the hell would I do?"

"You come in on this thing and help me out."

"I don't have money for that," Sammy says.

The fucker's actually gonna make this poor bastard say the words.

"It'll be my money," Kirby says." You just come on and oversee things."

"What do I know about pawn shops?" Sammy says. He looks at me. "Nothing, that's what."

"Just hear me out," Kirby says. "You just make sure I don't get robbed or run out of business. If there are any problems, you take care of 'em. Leave all the money to me. It'll be my money."

"If you're gonna get all the money, then why should I come in?"

"No, no, you misunderstand," Kirby says. "I put all the money in and take care of stuff. I pay the bills. You just make sure nobody messes with me. You do that, I'll give you ten percent of everything."

"That isn't what I do," Sammy says. "I'm a fucking minister, for God's sake."

"Just consider it. You come in and have the guys oversee everything."

"And I do what? Sit back and count my money?"

"You make sure I don't have problems," Kirby says. "And maybe help me get rid of the competition. Right now, there's five pawn shops in town. If I could get rid of a couple, I would make a lot more money. And that would be more money for you."

Sammy is nodding, thinking. Then he says, "Twenty percent."

Kirby looks nervous and unhappy. "Okay, okay, twelve percent."

"Seventeen."

"Fifteen," Kirby says.

"Every month?"

"Yeah."

Sammy wags his finger at him. "I'm telling you now, you're gonna have to have my money every month, no matter what. That's the only way this works."

"What happens if it's a bad month and I don't got the money?"

Sammy shrugs, smiling. "Just have it."

Kirby considers. "Okay, sure."

"And I don't put any money into the business?" Sammy asks.

"Not a dime."

"Are you sure you want this? I'm not a pawnbroker, Kirby."

"I think you could really help me," Kirby says. "I think we could make some real money here."

Sammy sits quietly an uncomfortably long time, pretending to mull it over. Then he puts his hand out for Kirby to shake. Kirby stands and approaches him, shaking his hand.

"Welcome to the pawn business," Kirby says.

Welcome to getting fucked, Kirby.

THIRTY-SEVEN

It's a Sunday afternoon in September. Cutter and I are at my place watching the Chiefs play the Raiders. I'm rooting for the Chiefs, but Cutter is a fucking Raiders fan. I don't mind that he hurts and kills people and does all kinds of other awful, heinous shit, but his being a Raiders fan makes it hard to be friends with him. The Chiefs are up by ten in the second quarter when someone knocks on the door.

I look at Cutter. "Jesus Christ, I'm trying to watch the game."

"Your boys are gonna lose anyway," Cutter says. "You might as well answer it."

When I open the door, a fat mountain of a man named Sheriff Lou Brehmer is standing there. I look around to see if Brehmer's got backup, but it's just him. Brehmer is the guy who replaced Virgil Jessup after Cutter made him disappear. Brehmer's nothing like Virgil. Brehmer's a tough S.O.B. who wants to put us all behind bars. He's been hounding us for the past year about Virgil's disappearance. Since everyone knew Virgil was dirty and working for Sammy, Brehmer thinks we had something to do with his disappearance.

Despite being a hard-ass, Brehmer's not so by-the-book that he doesn't still come by once a month to collect his payoff. He shakes all of Sammy's goons down, ransacking our houses and asking questions. It's all just a ruse for him to collect cash from us so he won't actually *do* anything.

He looks past me at Cutter. "How's the game going?"

"Not too bad," I say. "Chiefs are up by ten in the second."

"Who's got the ball?" Brehmer asks.

"The Raiders, but they haven't been able to do anything. All they've got so far is a field goal."

"There's still time," Brehmer says.

I squint at him. "I don't suspect you came all the way out here just to talk football."

"I don't suspect I did," Brehmer says. "Can I come in?"

I step aside. "Sure." Brehmer steps into the double-wide and looks at Cutter. "I'll be over to your place in a bit, Cutter. You gonna be there?"

Cutter grins. "Since I'm here and the game ain't even halfway over, I don't think I will. I haven't quite mastered that being-in-two-places-at-the-same-time shit."

"Will the missus be there?"

Cutter nods. "She will be, but don't give her too much of a hard time. She ain't like us. She's a nice girl."

Brehmer chuckles. "Yeah, right." I look at Cutter and see the remark's got his feathers ruffled. Cutter is still pissed that almost every good old boy in Taney County has either watched Kammie dance naked or has stuck their dick in one or more of her holes. Cutter lets the remark go and watches the game.

Brehmer goes straight to the drawer in the living room where he knows the envelope containing his money is. He slides it open, takes out the envelope, and stuffs it into his jacket. He turns and looks at me. "You know I've gotta ransack the place," he says. "To make it look good."

"Yeah, yeah," Cutter says. "Who would even know? Ain't nobody here."

Brehmer winks at him. "But I'd know, and that ain't my style."

"But takin' payoffs is?"

I don't say anything because it will do no good. All that will happen is that I'll either end up in jail or Brehmer will end up lying in the ground next to Virgil. I don't feel like going to jail, and I don't feel like digging. It's too cold for that shit.

Brehmer is opening the cabinets and spilling shit out onto the floor. Then he's rifling through the drawers, flipping papers and ink pens and all kinds of other loose stuff out onto the carpet. Then he moves on into the kitchen so he can repeat the process. Once the whole house is trashed, Brehmer says, "Have you boys come any closer to figuring out what might have happened to Virgil Jessup?"

Cutter looks at him. "This shit again?"

"We're still trying to find him," Brehmer says. "Virgil's got a family who's worried sick about him."

Cutter laughs. "Virgil was a goddamn degenerate. I don't know what happened to him, but his family shouldn't shed a single tear. Not one. That guy didn't give a shit about his family. Hell, he probably found himself a woman and ran off with her. I'll bet he's somewhere down south, across the border, banging some senorita half his age."

Brehmer stares at Cutter, considering it. "You might be right."

"I'm glad you recognize that," Cutter says. "Now, will you kindly get the fuck outta here so we can watch this goddamn game?"

As Brehmer heads for the door, he looks at me. "You should find better friends, Bill."

THIRTY-EIGHT

Sammy has called Cracker Jack, Cutter, and me into his trailer to discuss Branson Pawn. Cutter mentioned Sheriff Brehmer asking about Virgil again, which angered Sammy. Lately Sammy's been doing a fuck-ton of meth and he's been acting more and more erratic, so now he's completely unhinged.

He's sitting behind the table wagging his finger angrily at us. "Let me tell you something," he says. "That motherfucker Brehmer'll leave us alone if he knows what's good for himself. He takes our money, but he keeps askin' questions. Why do we even give him money if he's still gonna do his job? We pay him money *not* to do it."

"Typical pig move," Cutter says.

"Right, right," Cracker Jack says. "Typical pig move. It's getting where you can't even trust a cop to take the money and shut up. They want their goddamn cake and eat it too."

I'm not saying shit, but I wish Cracker Jack and Cutter would stop talking about all this because it only gets Sammy worked up. Before long he's gonna order Cracker Jack to go out and kill the sheriff, which is something we don't need. Especially after Virgil and Jeremy. There are only so many cops who can disappear around here before somebody important starts nosing around. I never really considered us cop killers because we killed Virgil and Jeremy for personal reasons, not because they were cops. But this would be different.

Sammy does another line of crank off the table, sits back, sniffles a bit, and turns to Cracker Jack. "I think you should do something about this pig." Cracker Jack is still killing folks for Sammy, but only the local ones. Sammy uses Gummy, the albino fucker, to do the ones outside the area.

Cracker Jack nods. Before he can say anything, I speak up. "I don't think this is a good idea. With all due respect, we can't be killing cops willy-nilly. It's eventually gonna bring a bunch of heat back on us, and we can't afford to have everything get shut down."

Sammy stares at me with a blank expression, and I'm curious which way this is gonna go. Is he gonna go along with me, or is it gonna piss him off that I've challenged him?

Cutter speaks up. "If any more pigs go missing around Taney County, somebody's gonna take notice. You know, an indordinant number."

"What's that mean?" Sammy asks.

"Indordinant," Cutter repeats.

"No, no," I say, "*inordinate.*"

"That's not right," Cutter says. "I think it's indordinant."

Cracker Jack says, "You want me to look it up on my phone? I can look it up."

I look at Sammy. "He's saying 'too many'. If too many cops disappear, the FBI's gonna come sniffing around, and we don't need that." I pause. "*You* don't need that."

Sammy leans back, puffing his cigar, considering this. He looks at me. "You might be right, kid."

"So, what then?" Cracker Jack asks.

"We wait," Sammy says. "See if Brehmer backs off." He turns and looks at me. "Let's talk about the pawn shop. How's that going?"

"Right as rain," I say.

"It's good then?"

Cutter nods. "So far, we've just been running up Kirby's credit, but we're about to take it to the next level. We're gonna break in and rob the place."

THIRTY-NINE

Tonight's the robbery. I've made sure the recorder connected to the surveillance system has been "accidentally" unplugged. When Kirby asks me about it later, I'll tell him I must have bumped it when I was vacuuming. Is that a good explanation? Probably not, but fuck Kirby, fuck the plug-in, and fuck Branson Pawn. Kirby can eat a dick for all I care.

There are bars on the windows, so we're going through a hole we've cut into the side of the building. It's Cutter, Rahmi, Cunny Jaymes, and me, carrying DVD players, books of old coins, televisions, guns, and video game systems out and loading them into a truck on the dark side street. After a while Cutter and I are just standing here, leaning on the truck and smoking our cigarettes, watching Rahmi and Cunny load the truck.

"This poor bastard had no idea what he was getting into when he asked Sammy to come be his partner," Cutter says, chuckling.

I chuckle too. "It's like inviting Harvey Weinstein to sleep in your bed and expecting him not to try any crazy shit."

"That's right," Cutter says. "Kirby doesn't get to play like he's the poor put-upon victim. He asked for this shit. He *begged* for this."

I change the subject. "How are things with Kammie? She still mad?"

Kammie found a dirty rubber under their bed a few days ago. Cutter doesn't use a rubber with her, so she's understandably pissed. At first, he said it wasn't his. He actually suggested that someone might have broken in and left the rubber there. But then he tried a different approach, telling her she should be happy he was being safe when he cheated. Needless to say, this didn't go over well.

"She ain't too happy," Cutter says. "But she'll get over it. It's like my grandmother used to say—'she'll get glad in the same pants she got mad in.'"

I look at him. "That shit don't make no sense."

Cutter waves it off. "Kammie thinks I should let her screw somebody to make up for it. No way in hell is that happening." He chuckles. "That'll be the fuckin' day!"

I don't tell Cutter that she texted this same thing to me, and I *really* don't tell him she said she wanted the guy to be me. Of course, I would never do that anyway. I love Grace and I don't wanna cheat on her, and I also love Cutter and don't wanna hurt him. Besides, I've already screwed Kammie once and she wasn't all that great to begin with. She's not even my type. She's decent-looking, sure, but she's terrible, both as a human being and as a lay. So Kammie doesn't like me too much right now either. You'd think she'd learn to stop trying to screw me, but she keeps trying. Not a week goes by that she doesn't send me at least one come-fuck-me text.

Cutter says, "If she keeps talkin' that shit, she's gonna make me go fuck some more bitches."

We both chuckle. We both know he's gonna do it anyway.

At this moment, a Sheriff's Department cruiser emerges from the alley across the street. The cop just sits there for a moment, watching us. Then he edges out of the alley and moves slowly, almost idling, towards us. We're standing in front of the truck and the driver's side window of the cruiser is down. It comes a little closer and we see that it's Brehmer. He sidles up beside us and I know Rahmi and Cunny

132

are gonna pop out from the side of the pawn shop with their arms full of stolen shit at any moment.

"What are you guys doing here?" Brehmer asks.

"We came to get something," Cutter says.

Brehmer's eyes narrow. "What's that?"

"This," Cutter says, raising his arm, revealing a hunting knife. Before either Brehmer or I know what's happening, Cutter shoves the knife deep into Brehmer's eye. Brehmer screams a scream that gives me chills. The handle of the knife is sticking out of Brehmer's eye and he's thrashing around like a wounded animal. There's blood all over the car, the seat, the window, everywhere. Now the car starts idling forward. Apparently Brehmer had it in drive with his foot on the brake, and when Cutter stabbed him, his foot came off.

"What the fuck?!" Cutter screams.

The cruiser idles forward and hits the truck, but it doesn't make much sound. The truck rocks and moves a tiny bit from the impact, but the cruiser is momentarily stopped, although it's still trying to move forward. Brehmer's still technically alive, thrashing around. I grab the door handle and swing the driver's side door open. I reach in and grab the knife, twisting it hard and jamming it in a bit. Brehmer twitches a little and dies. I shove his body over into the passenger seat. "I'll take the cop car out to the boat ramp!" I say. "Pack these guys up and meet me out there ASAP!"

I climb inside, my ass sliding in slick, wet blood, and I shut the door. I look at Cutter. "Fucking hurry. I don't wanna get caught with a stolen cruiser that's got a dead sheriff inside."

FORTY

I'M TRYING to avoid being seen, so I take the back streets. Somehow, I make it out of the city without any bullshit. I'm inclined to stomp on the gas and speed, but I don't wanna raise any red flags. I'm as nervous as Donald Trump taking a lie detector test. I sweat a lot anyway, and now I'm sweating buckets. My Metallica shirt is drenched like a kid playing in the sprinkler. There's some chatter on the radio and the dispatcher asks Brehmer what he's up to. "You ain't over there fuckin' Colleen Dandridge again, are you?" the female dispatcher asks. "Your wife has called twice." When Brehmer doesn't answer, the dispatcher stops talking.

I'm terrified every time I see a car. I feel conspicuous, like there's sign on the car telling people I'm a cop killer. I glance over at Brehmer to make sure he's still dead and, yep, still dead.

My ringtone starts going off in my pocket. It's "Feel Like Making Love," letting me know it's Grace. I fish the phone from my pocket. I ponder whether or not I should answer. Finally, I do.

"Hey, Gracie Girl," I say, trying to sound calm.

"Where are you?" she asks.

"I'm busy, babe."

There's a pause. "Are you fucking somebody, Billy?"

"Of course not."

"You sound funny."

Of course I do. I'm driving a stolen cop car complete with a dead sheriff in the passenger seat. I defy a motherfucker to do this and not sound funny. But there's nothing funny about any of it.

"I promise you everything is fine," I say.

"Do you have a woman with you?"

"Don't be silly," I say. "I don't cheat."

"Cutter cheats on Kammie, and he's your best friend."

"Well, it's Kammie," I say. "If I was with her, I'd cheat too."

I expect her to laugh, but she doesn't.

"So, you would cheat?"

"It was a joke."

"Where the fuck are you?" She's angry now.

I'm looking in the rearview at a pair of headlights zipping up from the darkness behind. Sweat snakes down my forehead and into my eye, causing it to burn. I blink, still watching the headlights.

"I promise," I say. "It's just work."

"If you loved me, you'd tell me the truth."

"There are certain things I just can't tell you. But I promise, it's not a woman."

"How can I trust you?"

"Look, Gracie Girl, I'll level with you. I'm doing work shit right now. You know what I do. Well, a work thing just went sideways, and it's bad."

"How bad?"

"I don't wanna worry you. Just go to bed and I'll be home as soon as I can."

"Talk to me, Billy. How bad is it?"

I look over at Brehmer. "Okay, look, it's bad enough that there's a dead guy sitting next to me."

"Oh, my God," she says. There's a pause. "Did you... kill him?"

"No," I say. We've never discussed my killing anyone, but I can tell her the truth this once.

"You sound like you're driving."

"I am."

"Did you get blood on the seats?"

I almost laugh. "It's somebody else's car."

"Okay," she says. "That's good, I guess." She pauses. "The dead guy..."

"Yeah?"

"It's not Cutter, is it?"

"No, baby, it's not anyone like that."

"No one I know?"

"Not really," I say.

"What does that mean?"

"No one who's a friend."

"Just do me a favor," she says.

"What's that?"

"Be careful."

"I promise, baby. But I need to go. I've got to take care of this."

"You won't get in trouble?" She's on the verge of tears. "I don't wanna raise Gilbert alone."

"No, baby, I won't get in trouble. I'm gonna get rid of the car and the body."

"How?"

I don't want to tell her that I'm gonna sink Brehmer and the cruiser deep under Table Rock Lake. Instead I say, "Don't worry your pretty little head. I've got things under control."

FORTY-ONE

THE NEXT DAY I'm exhausted. Brehmer and the cruiser are both under water and somehow Cutter and I managed to not get caught putting them there. I'm at Branson Pawn and Kirby is upset. He's leaning against the near-empty glass case crying with one of his hands over his eyes. He lowers it and looks at me. "This place is all I got."

"Don't worry," I say. "We'll find the motherfuckers who robbed us. Nobody steals from Reverend Sammy and gets away with it." Of course, this is all bullshit since we stole the shit.

Kirby looks exhausted. The poor bastard has been crying for hours. "I can't believe this," he says. "Who would do this, Bill? You know me, I'm a good guy. I don't deserve this."

"It ain't about deserving it," I say. "Criminals don't care who they rob. All they care about is making a quick buck."

"I'm well aware," Kirby says, looking at me in a way that suggests he's suspicious. "You know, the surveillance camera was off."

"The cameras don't work?"

"Not the cameras. The cameras worked, but they didn't record anything." He pauses, staring at me. "Somehow the recorder got *unplugged*. You know anything about that?"

137

I feign ignorance. "You think I had something to do with this?"

"No, no," Kirby says, backtracking. "I just meant that you and me are the only ones who go in the office, and I never unplug it."

I play it off. "I don't know," I say. "I mighta unplugged it when I was vacuuming."

He looks at me with a confused expression. I can tell he doesn't believe me but fuck him. Who cares? This is what he gets for bringing us in. When you swim with sharks, your ass gets eaten.

"I sure hope this doesn't happen again," he says, still staring at me. "I would hate to have to get violent."

"I get you, Kirby. I would hate to have to bash somebody's head the fuck in, if you know what I mean." I say it forcefully without taking my eyes away from his.

"You mean the robbers, right?"

"Whoever, Kirby. Whoever the fuck it applies to."

FORTY-TWO

YEAR SIX

It's a snowy day in January when Sammy tells us he's decided to end his partnership with Kirby. It's me, Cutter, Cracker Jack, and Sammy —the usual suspects—sitting at a table in the fellowship hall of the First Redeemer Church. Normally we would have met in Sammy's trailer, but today he's having it swept for bugs.

Sammy is leaning over the table with his hands on it, and he shrugs, opening his palms. "It is finished."

Cracker Jack squints at him. "What's finished?"

"Those were Jesus' last words before he died."

"So what? You gonna die?"

"It's time for us to get out of the pawn business."

I'm lighting my cigarette. I take a couple puffs before I ask, "What's the plan? We gonna burn the place down?"

"This is the genius part," Sammy says, tapping his temple. "Burning it down is obvious. The insurance company will be all over that. But I got a different way. I like to think outside the box, so I was thinking we could set off the sprinklers."

"What sprinklers?" Cutter asks.

Sammy points upwards. "The overhead sprinklers."

"The ones in the store?" Cracker Jack asks.

"No, the ones at your mother's house," Cutter says, grinning.

We all ignore this.

"They got sprinklers up there," Sammy says. "Kirby wouldn't even let me smoke in there."

Cracker Jack nods. "I remember."

"Okay, so we light something under 'em and set 'em off. Then they come on and spray water everywhere, ruining all the inventory. Then we cut our losses and take our cut of Kirby's insurance payout."

The conversation is interrupted when Cracker Jack asks Cutter, "Why the fuck you scratchin' your nuts like that?" We all look and see Cutter stopped motionless with his hand hovering over his junk.

"Why don't you mind your fuckin' business?"

"What?" Cracker Jack says. "You got crabs or something?"

Cutter glares at him, his hand still on his balls. "I don't wanna talk about it."

"I'll bet."

I chuckle. Sammy doesn't give a shit about any of it and continues. "I figure we lean on Kirby to give us a cut of the money."

"More than the normal fifteen percent?" I ask.

"Way more."

"What if he doesn't like that?"

"Then fuck him," Sammy says. "He can go along to get along, or he can get fucked like a two-dollar hooker on Saturday night."

We all nod.

"I don't feel bad for him," I say. "He shoulda known."

"He should have," Sammy says. Then he looks over at Cutter, digging at his nuts again. "What the fuck, man?"

Cutter looks up. "What do you want from me? I got fuckin' crabs, okay? It ain't like none of you ever had 'em before."

"Take your ass to Walgreens and get some ointment," Sammy growls. "Then you chuckle-fucks go set off the sprinklers and put Kirby out of business."

FORTY-THREE

It's the middle of the night. Cutter and me are driving to the pawn shop to do the deed. Cutter looks over and says, "Did you hear about Bill White?" I'm driving but I turn to look at him.

"What about him?"

"You ain't gonna believe this," Cutter says. "The fuckin' prick is runnin' for President."

"President of what?" I ask. "Of the *country*?"

"One and the same."

This sounds like bullshit, so I ask, "Where'd you hear that?"

"It's everywhere," Cutter says. "It's all over the news."

"Since when do you watch the news?"

"Never, but I get news reports on my phone," he says. "I mostly ignore 'em unless they're sports, but this one stood out."

"What'd it say?"

Cutter shrugs. "It said he's running for President, whaddaya think?"

"Huh. What do you think about that?"

Cutter grins. "I think it's gonna be harder to rob him next time."

I laugh. "I ain't never voted before, but..."

He looks at me. "What?"

"I feel bad for the poor dumb bastard. Maybe I'll vote for him."

"You think that'll make up for what we done?" he asks. "You think your lame-ass vote is worth three million bucks?"

I grin. "Maybe I'll send him a fruit basket."

"You know what?" Cutter asks. "You *are* a fruit basket."

FORTY-FOUR

It's been three months since the sprinklers went off inside Branson Pawn, destroying everything. We're meeting with Kirby again, discussing what Sammy calls "the particulars." This time is different than the previous meetings. This time we're on top of the Radisson. Sammy is talking to Kirby, and Cutter and me are holding Kirby upside down by his ankles.

"You disgust me, Kirby," Sammy says.

Kirby doesn't say anything. He's just crying and whimpering.

"What?" Sammy says. "You're not gonna say nothing?"

Cutter growls at Kirby. *"You better talk, you degenerate fuck!"*

"I didn't know I was supposed to talk!" Kirby says.

"Billy says you told him you're not gonna give me half of the money you're getting," Sammy says. "Is that true?"

"I'm sorry!"

"Oh, you're sorry alright," I say.

"I think the exact quote was, 'Tell Sammy to go fuck himself,'" Sammy says. "Is that what you think of me? That I'm somebody who can go fuck himself?"

Kirby screams something defensive and unrecognizable.

Sammy looks down at him. "That what you think, you piece of shit?"

"*No!*"

"You know what's stopping me from letting them drop you?"

Kirby is sobbing hard.

"You better answer when he speaks!" Cutter says.

Before Kirby can, Sammy is talking again. "The money. That's it. I asked for half, which is $78,000. And you did *what?* You told me to go fuck myself, Kirby. So now it's gonna be an even hundred."

"No, please!" Kirby wails, somehow more afraid of losing the money than his life.

"Oh, yes," Sammy says. "I need the money by the end of the week. Do you hear me, you fuck?"

"I- I... can't!"

"What the fuck did you say?" Cracker Jack growls.

"They said it could be ninety days before I get the money!"

Sammy looks at him. "You're gonna pay me before that. Then you can pay yourself back when you get the money. How you like that?"

"I can't. I... I don't have it."

"Then you'd better get it!" Cutter says.

"Listen," says Sammy, "there's two ways we can do this. The easy way, or the you-die-a-horrible-ghastly-fucking-death way. Which way's it gonna be?"

Kirby is bawling his ass off.

"My guys are gonna come see you at the end of the week," Sammy says.

Kirby interrupts. "It's already Tuesday. I don't even get a full week?"

"Be thankful for what you get," Sammy says. "When they visit, your ass had better have $100,000 in cash."

"What if I can't get it?"

"If you're even a dime short, we'll drag you back up here," Sammy says. "If you got $99,999.99, we'll still bring you back. Only next time we won't be so nice. Next time Cutter and Billy are gonna drop you headfirst onto the pavement. You ever see what a head looks like when it falls onto pavement from this high up?"

"No," Kirby manages.

Sammy giggles. "And you don't wanna. Don't make us come back up here."

"No," Cutter says. "*Please do.* Because I wanna drop you. I wanna drop you *so bad.* Right on top of your big fat stupid head, Kirby!"

"He means it," Cracker Jack says. "Cutter loves this shit."

Cutter giggles maniacally now. "You know what, Kirbs? He's right. I do."

Sammy asks, "So what are you gonna do, Kirby?"

"I'm gonna have your money."

"How much?"

"$100,000."

"That's right," Sammy says. "And when are you gonna have it?"

"Sunday?" Kirby asks.

"No, motherfucker," Sammy says. "Friday. You have that money by Friday afternoon or you're gonna be one dead pawnshop owner fuck."

FORTY-FIVE

I WAS all night burying Travis. You remember him, right? He was the kid who wanted to come work for Sammy. Instead he got chopped up and buried in the woods. Maybe he's lucky. Maybe death is better than working at Funland. All in all, Funland ain't so bad, but Sammy is a fucking loon these days and that makes the job suck. Somehow, I don't mind Cutter's lunacy nearly as much as Sammy's. Maybe it's because Cutter is actually the one carrying out the acts of violence and not just some fat pussy sitting in a trailer getting head from ugly bitches and ordering murders. That's a key distinction. This is why people have more respect for the soldiers who fight wars than the fat fuck presidents who start them.

I'm in Branson checking in on some of our businesses. I'm hungry, so I stop at this barbecue place I like. A mom and pop place called The Piggy Pen. Stupid name, but the food is on point. I always get the same thing—a fried bologna sandwich, fried corn on the cob, and baked beans.

I get the food and sit by the window, reflecting on my life choices. I don't know why, but killing Travis seemed worse than some of the others. Don't get me wrong, none of them were good, but this kid didn't do anything, and now he's worm food. All because Sammy's meth addiction is out of control and has him seeing shit where it don't exist.

I'm sitting here thinking, and this asshole in an off-the-rack Sears suit comes over to my table. I didn't even see him come in. I look up at the guy—probably forty, no facial hair, generic in every way. He's not even carrying food. "Can I sit with you?" he asks.

"I ain't no fag."

"I didn't think you were, Billy."

I stare at him, trying to figure him out. Who the fuck is he? So, I ask him.

He sits down across from me and folds his hands on the table. "Who do you think I am?"

I look him over. "I figure you for a cop."

"Close, but not quite."

I take a bite of my sandwich, trying to pretend I'm not spooked. He opens his jacket and pulls out a wallet, showing me his FBI badge.

"Am I supposed to be impressed?" I ask.

He grins. "How you been, Billy?"

"What do you want?"

He points his finger at my face. "You got barbecue sauce right there on your chin."

"Maybe I like it there." I don't wipe it away.

"Suit yourself," he says. "We know who you work for."

"It's no secret. I work at Funland. I work the dunk tank."

"That pay well?" he asks.

"*Asi asi,*" I say.

He raises his eyebrows. "You speak Spanish?"

"Mostly just curse words."

"Well, I figured you must get paid pretty well. You got a nice new double-wide, right there next to your Mexican pal." He pauses. "Musta been him who taught you the Spanish."

I just shrug as I go to work on the fried corn on the cob.

He smirks. "You're just gonna leave that sauce on your chin?"

"Do you see me wiping it off?"

We make eye contact. He wants me to see that he's serious now. "We're gonna catch your boss, Billy. I think we both know that. What you need to decide is, how's that gonna work for you? Are you gonna help us catch him, or are you gonna end up behind bars and getting fucked in the ass right there next to him?"

I play dumb. "I don't know what you're talking about."

"I think you do."

"Well, you thinking it doesn't make it a thing."

He reaches into his pocket and pulls out his wallet again. He fishes out a business card and slides it across the table. It says SPECIAL AGENT DOUGLAS WARNER. I smirk. "Douglas Warner? That's a weenie name." I toss the card, spiraling it back at him. It hits his chest and bounces off, falling to the floor.

"You'd better keep the card," he says. "If you're smart, you'll call and make a deal."

He stands to leave, and I say, "No one ever said I was smart."

"Now that, I believe." And he strides out.

"Fuckin' pig," I mutter.

A moment later I pick up my tray and go dump it. I'm about to leave when I stop and return to the table. I lean down and pick up the business card.

FORTY-SIX

"Kammie wants to try for another kid," Cutter says from behind the steering wheel. "But I don't wanna."

"So, what are you gonna do?" I ask.

"I'm just gonna fuck her in the ass. Then I won't have to worry about it."

"You're a real romantic."

"You know," he says, "this marriage stuff ain't what I thought it would be."

"Yeah?"

"Yeah," he says. "I still love her, but she's a real pain in the ass. She's always bustin' my balls, accusing me of fuckin' other women. I hate that shit."

"But you do fuck other women."

He groans. "I know, okay? But she don't know. It's the principle. I hate being accused of shit she don't know for a fact I'm doing."

"But you do it!"

He turns and looks at me with fire in his eyes. "I know it and you know it, but she don't, okay? So, it's unfair of her to accuse me! It's bullshit and it pisses me off! And if you keep challenging me, *you're* gonna piss me off!"

I could argue with him further, but Cutter's never gonna get it. It's not that he's too stupid to get it, it's that he doesn't want to get it. And I don't need him having a meltdown over some stupid shit. I've got enough problems as it is.

We pull up in front of Kirby's house. His truck isn't there.

Cutter looks at me. "You think he's here?"

I shrug. "I got the same information you got."

We get out and walk up to the house. Cutter knocks on the door. As we wait, he turns and looks at me. He's punching his fist into the inside of his other hand. "I hope this cocksucker's light. I'd love to punch his face in."

"What's Kirby ever done to you?"

"I guess he's just got a punchable face."

"You think everybody's got a punchable face."

Cutter nods. "This is true."

When Kirby doesn't answer, I reach for my phone. "Lemme call him."

The phone rings five times and goes to voicemail. The message plays and Kirby sounds happy-go-lucky like he doesn't have a care in the world. I leave him a message. "Hey Kirby, it's me, Bill. We're at your house, but you ain't here. We're wondering where you are. Do us both a favor; call me when you get this."

I click off.

Cutter looks at me. "You think he's gonna call back?"

"No," I say. "I think he's in the wind."

FORTY-SEVEN

Two MONTHS PASS before Kirby turns up. That's quite a while and I've gotta say I'm impressed he was able to hide that long. When he turns up, he's hiding out in a motel in Kimberling City.

Cracker Jack and Cutter went to Joplin to meet with one of our associates. But then Sammy got news that Kirby was in Kimberling City, so he sent me. "We don't know how long he's gonna be there," Sammy said, "so I need you to get over there today and take care of him." I asked Sammy if he was sure he wanted me to kill him since we hadn't gotten the insurance money yet, but Sammy was spun out and angry. He gave me a throwaway .45 and said, "You kill that cocksucker, and you kill him good." So now I'm on way to see Kirby.

I'm driving when the phone rings. I hold it up and look at it, but I don't recognize the number. I'd like to ignore it, but you never know when it's gonna be business. Business means money, and I can't ignore money.

"Who's this?"

"I'll give you two guesses," Kammie says.

"What do you want?"

"I want you," she says. "Why won't you fuck me, Billy? Come on. At least let me suck you off."

"We've been through this," I say. "It's not gonna happen."

"Don't you think I look good? Am I not pretty enough for you?"

"I love Grace."

"Cutter cheats on me," she says. "Why won't you cheat on Grace?"

I want to tell her it's because I'm not a scumbag, but I don't. Instead I say, "I'm not like that."

"What are you like?"

I click off the phone, thinking, that's what I'm like.

The phone immediately starts ringing again, but I switch off the ringer and turn up the stereo.

Twenty minutes later, I'm in Kimberling City, making my way to the Tropic Motel. The Tropic Motel is a rundown flophouse that looks like it was probably nice when my grandpa was young. But it looks like shit now. The paint job is pink, and the bricks even manage to look outdated. I pull the Blazer into the empty parking lot and park right out front. I walk into the office.

A fat dude with a blonde beard who looks to be in his younger forties steps out from the backroom. He's got his mouth full and he's chewing. Whatever he's eating must be greasy because he wipes his hands on his NASCAR shirt, leaving orange streaks. "Can I help you?"

"You Kevin?"

He furrows his brow, and his mouth twists up. "That depends on who you are."

"You know Reverend Sammy?"

He relaxes. "Oh," he says. "I thought maybe you was a cop."

"I sure as shit am not a cop."

"Good," he says. "Can't say I like cops much."

"How many people are staying here?" I ask.

Kevin laughs. "Are you kidding? No one. No one is here except

152

for your guy. No one ever stays here unless all the other places are full."

"Sammy said you'd have a key."

Kevin nods and turns toward a wall with keys hanging on it. He plucks one off, turning towards me. I hold out my palm and he drops the key into it.

"Room 27," he says.

I look around. "You got surveillance cameras here?"

He laughs. "Nothing here's been updated since before surveillance cameras. In fact, I'd venture to guess nothing has been updated since before the guy who invented surveillance cameras was born."

I reach for the .45 I've got tucked in my waistband.

"You gonna kill the guy?" he asks, looking eager.

I raise the gun and stick it in his face. His eyes get big and I squeeze the trigger. Suddenly he doesn't look so eager.

FORTY-EIGHT

I STROLL out of the office, not even bothering to hide the gun. I look at the numbers on the doors and make my way to Kirby's room. I go up to the door, stop, and look around, seeing no one. With the pistol raised, I unlock the door. I then push the door open to find Kirby sitting naked at the desk, mid-jerk, watching porn on his laptop. He stops jerking and stares at me with his mouth agape. The door shuts behind me and the room gets dark.

"You wanna fuck me, don't you, daddy?" asks a porn chick on Kirby's laptop.

"Oh, uh, hey...," says Kirby.

"Why did you run?"

Kirby raises his hand from his dick and swivels his chair to face me.

"*Jesus Christ!*" I say. "I don't wanna see your pecker."

"Don't kill me," Kirby says.

"Do you like my tits, daddy?" asks the porn chick.

"Do you have the money?" I ask.

Kirby looks confused, but to be fair, there's a lot happening. "What?"

I reposition the gun to show him I mean business.

"The insurance money," I say. "Do you have it?"

"No." He shakes his head like a little boy. "I haven't got it yet."

"Too bad."

I'm about to pull the trigger when Kirby says, "Maybe we can make a deal."

I humor him. "What kinda deal?"

His eyes move down my body. "I could suck your dick," he says. "What do you think of that?"

"Suck on this," I say as I squeeze the trigger.

FORTY-NINE

I HOLD up the electronic keychain remote and hit the button, but the Blazer doors don't unlock. "Shit," I mutter. I sit the phone on top of the Blazer and fumble with the keys. I unlock the door and climb inside. I turn on the ignition and Megadeath's "Wake Up Dead" comes on. I turn the vehicle around and go to drive out of the lot. I'm waiting for traffic to clear so I can pull out when a burgundy SUV pulls in. As the SUV passes, the blonde woman driving looks at me.

Well, shit. This could be a problem.

I pull out into the street, stressing over the woman as I do. Fuck it, maybe it's not a big deal. But it kind of is because I'm driving in my own Blazer. I drive a couple blocks before it occurs to me to message Kammie to tell her to leave me alone. I reach for my phone and realize I don't have it. Now it dons on me that I left it on top of the Blazer. Dammit! I pull over, trying to do it slowly so the phone won't fall if it's still on top of the vehicle. I get out and look, but the phone is gone. I stand there for a moment, looking back down the busy street. The phone could be anywhere.

Now a second thought occurs to me: what if the phone fell off in the motel parking lot? If the cops find that, they'll have a field day. I climb into the Blazer, turn around and head back, making a point to watch for the phone in the street, but I don't see it. There's a dip as the motel entrance meets the street, so I figure that's where it slid off. But it's not there, making me pull back into the lot. But it's okay because this will allow me to kill two birds with one stone.

When I pull back into the lot, I see the burgundy SUV parked next to the office. The woman is beside the office entrance, smoking a cigarette, probably trying to finish it before going in. I sidle up beside the SUV, which I now see is a Cutlass. I open the door and get out. I approach the woman.

"How are you?" she asks nonchalantly.

I raise the .45 and fire. I want to shoot her in the face, but I'm walking, which causes me to miss and shoot her in the throat. The cigarette falls from her mouth and her hands reach for her neck. She topples back hard onto the pavement, flopping around like a fish out of water. I step forward and fire a round into her nose, making a mess of her face. She stops flailing and I turn to look for my phone. I see it lying on the pavement. As I walk towards it, it begins to ring again.

FIFTY

It's BEEN three weeks since I clipped Kirby. Nothing came of it and nobody ever came and questioned anyone at Funland. Like the rest of the bad shit we do, we're gonna get away with it. The carnys at Funland are like kids; we do as much as we can get away with. Since we never get caught, we constantly raise the bar.

There's nothing special about today. It's just another Tuesday. I've got to go to Sammy's chop shop and check on things, make sure everything's on the up and up and Sammy's getting every dime he's supposed to. Then this evening I'll put on the clown makeup, climb inside the dunk tank, and say mean things to strangers. Just another day in paradise.

It's just before noon when I walk into the Kum-Quik convenience store, which is a couple miles from my house. I love the food here. Grace says it's nothing special and that it's just regular old gas station food, but she's wrong. I'm a connoisseur of gas station food, and the grub is top notch. My favorites are the little tacos and the bacon cheeseburger, but today I'm in the mood for a rib sandwich. Hopefully, they've got one. Some days they're either out of them or the minimum wage monkeys who work the counter just forget to make them.

I go to the glass case and peer in. To my delight, I see three foil-covered rib sandwiches. But now that I'm here, the pork sandwich catches my eye. But I've gotta take a leak, so the decision will have to wait. I stroll into the john, thankful it's empty. I step up the urinal, pull out Little Billy, and let him hang. There's no one here, so the urine flows freely. The door behind me opens and a man's voice says, "Hey there, sexy."

What the fuck? I turn around slightly but can only turn so far as I'm midstream, so I can't see who's behind me.

"I hope you ain't talking to me," I say.

"Do you see anybody else here?"

I finish, shake Little Billy off, and stuff him back in my boxers. Then I button up and turn to see the FBI guy standing there with a smirk on his face.

"What are you?" I say. "Some kinda fag?"

Special Agent Warner chuckles. "How you been, Billy?"

I walk past him to wash my hands.

"I think you should come in and talk to us," he says. "We can help you and your family."

There are no paper towels in the dispenser. I shake the water off my hands. "Maybe I'll come in if you can get me some paper towels."

Warner doesn't smile. He looks me in the eyes and says, "Does the name Kirby Carnahan ring any bells?"

I do a double take and I'm sure he sees the startled look on my face, but I try to play it off. "The only Kirby I know is the dead baseball player."

"No, I'm talking about the dead pawnbroker," Warner says. "Think hard. You know him."

I scrunch up my face, pretending I'm trying to remember. But then I think, fuck this pig. The fun thing about cops is that sometimes they know things, but they can't prove them. When that happens, you can fuck with them by exaggerating your responses condescendingly.

In other words, your words say "no", but your actions say "fuck yes, pig, what you gonna do about it?" So, I go with that. I grin big, letting my eyes tell him hell yeah, I know Kirby fucking Carnahan. But my mouth says, "Oh yeah, I think I met him once."

"Yeah?" Warner asks.

"I'm pretty sure I bought my wife's wedding ring off him."

Warner's eyebrow raises. "That all you know?"

"I think maybe he overcharged me."

"You remember anything else?"

"Nope, not a thing."

"You wanna know what I think?" Warner asks.

"Sure but make it quick. I wanna get out there and get a rib sandwich before they're all gone."

"I think Kirby was in business with Reverend Sammy."

"At Funland?" I ask.

His look doesn't waver. "Wanna know what else I think?"

I stare at him in silence. He says, "I think Sammy had him killed, and I think you know who killed him." He pauses. "In fact, I think it coulda been you or your spic pal."

I'm nervous, but I don't show it. "Get yourself some worms, Warner."

He gives me a confused look. "What's that supposed to mean?"

I wink at him. "It means you're fishing." I'm doing a pretty good job of pretending I'm not scared. I turn and walk out of the bathroom, feeling shaken. I go outside. As I'm climbing into the Blazer, Warner steps out and approaches me. He grins. "Hey, cool guy, I think you forgot something."

"Oh yeah? What's that?"

"I thought you were gonna get a rib sandwich."

FIFTY-ONE

YEAR SEVEN

I⊤'s a hot and humid May evening. Cutter and me are sitting outside his place in lawn chairs, drinking Natty Light, listening to music on Cutter's boombox, and giving our blood to the mosquitoes. Kammie's out with friends, so it's just us. Grace and Gil are gone, too. They've gone to visit Grace's folks in Springfield because her brother Steve has just been released from prison.

"You shoulda went with Grace," Cutter says. "You're supposed to do those things when you're married."

I take a drink. "I do most of the good husband shit, but Grace's folks don't like me. No matter what I do, I'm never gonna be good enough."

"Why don't they like you?"

"The regular stuff," I say. "The long hair. The fact that I come from white trash. And her dad thinks I'm a criminal."

Cutter chuckles. "He's right."

"True," I concede. "But it's like you say about Kammie thinkin' you're cheating. She's right, but she don't know she's right, so it's fucked up."

"Yeah, fuck Grace's dad."

"He makes good money."

"Oh yeah? What's he do?"

"The fucker insurance or some kinda shit like that," I say. "I always figure if Grace ever leaves me, I'm gonna go rob her folks."

"They got a nice house?"

"Yeah," I say. "Nice cars, nice house. Fuckers even got a boat."

"I want a boat," Cutter says.

"Me too."

"What? You gonna go skiing and shit?"

"Maybe I'll just go fishing."

"I don't figure you for a fisherman."

I shrug. "If I had a boat, I I'd just take it out and just have a good time floating around drinking beer."

Neither of us says anything for a while, both of us just listening to AC/DC's "High Voltage." I'm nodding my head, mumbling to the words, and Cutter says, "Do you like this life?"

"How do you mean?"

"All this criminal shit," he says. "Working for Sammy."

I shrug. "I don't think about it all that much. I just figure this is my lot in life. Some guys are doctors or firemen, and this... this is what we do. We work for Sammy, taking care his dirty work."

Cutter looks at me. "Don't that bother you, cleaning up his shit all the time?"

"I don't love it, but it is what it is."

"I get tired of it," Cutter says. "I don't mind hurtin' people—"

"You love it."

Cutter grins. "I do, but Sammy... Maybe it's just the beer talkin', but he's a rat fuck."

We both chuckle.

"I'm serious," he says. "The fucker's even got rat teeth. Little cheese-nibblers."

I laugh again.

He continues. "I think it's fucked up that he sends us out to do his shit because he's not man enough to do it himself."

"You think that?"

"I do," Cutter says. "I really do."

"I always figured he was pretty tough back in the day."

"But guess what?" Cutter says. "This ain't back in the day no more. I think he's using us, and I don't think he appreciates the shit we do. He pays us alright, but it's only a small fraction of what he sees. I swear he thinks this is the Mafia."

"I heard him say that once," I say. "Right after I started, he said Funland was the white trash mafia."

"He's a bitch," Cutter says. "Sometimes I think about hurting him."

This surprises me. "Really?"

"I think about it a lot. Because I can't respect a motherfucker who sends other people out to hurt people all the time. A man who does that ain't no man at all."

"I never thought of it like that."

"It's all I think about," Cutter says.

I know it's mostly the booze talking, but I can tell he means it. I don't care one way or the other, but I don't wanna see Cutter get in over his head. I don't have any allegiance to Sammy, but I know how all this would go down if Cutter challenged him. It would end up with Cutter being cut up and buried in the woods.

We sit and listen to the music. At some point, I fall asleep. When I wake up, Kammie is rubbing my dick. I sit up. "What the fuck?" I look at Cutter, who's asleep a few feet away.

Kammie is squatting in front of me. "He's not waking up anytime soon."

I grab her arm. "Don't do that."

She gives me a wounded look. "You know you want it."

She's right, I do. And she knows it because my dick is hard enough to cut glass, but I push her away, stand up, and go home.

FIFTY-TWO

A COUPLE WEEKS have passed since I woke to Kammie's hand on my crotch. She's calmed down some, which is good, but things are rough with Grace right now. Sometimes I think maybe I should have fucked Kammie, but I know that's bullshit. But damn, I try my hardest and shit is still a mess. No matter what I do, Grace and I end up fighting. We're in the middle of a screaming match when she looks at me with disgust and says, "This isn't what I wanted for Gilbert." She pauses. "It's not what I wanted for me either."

I stare at her, feeling stupid, unsure what to say. "What do you want, Grace? What can I possibly do to make your life better? I'm sorry I'm not some rich banker like your sister's husband, Dave or Jason or whatever the fuck his name is."

She glares at me. It's more than a glare. She's looking at me like I'm a huge pile of shit. *"Is that what you think I want, Billy? You think I want some dipshit banker who wears Dockers and loafers?"*

"Then what do you want?"

She stares at me for a long moment with a hard, angry look in her eyes. "I want a husband who doesn't do what you do for a living."

So, this is what it's about. She's never come right out and said it, but I've always known. Usually she bitches about everything else, from my staying out late to the bills to whatever else, but now she's actually saying it.

"What is it you think I do?" I ask.

"Don't make me laugh," she says. "You think I don't know?"

"Tell me what it is you think I do."

She glares at me with eyes so fiery I'm afraid I'll catch fire. "I think you do a lot of really fucked up shit. That's bad enough but doing it for someone else is even worse."

Now she sounds like Cutter, and I know she's either been talking to him or, more likely, Kammie. Either way, those words are Cutter's.

"What do you know about it?" I ask.

"I know plenty. I know you hurt people, Billy, and a lot more than that. I know you steal, and you lie, and you do all kinds of other really despicable shit."

"Who told you that?"

"Do you think I'm an idiot?" she laughs. "Is that what you think?"

I stare at her in silence, unsure what to say. She breaks the silence. "I'm tired of living this way. Either we get out of this life together, or Gil and I get out without you."

This hits me hard. I feel tired and deflated. "Is that an ultimatum?"

"What do you think?"

Gil is crying down the hall and Grace storms off to his room, leaving me alone. Alone with the realization that I'm about to lose the only good things I've ever known. I sit down on the floor with my hands over my face, crying.

This isn't life I wanted for our family either, but I don't know how to get us out.

FIFTY-THREE

I'M SITTING in Sammy's decrepit trailer with Cutter and Cracker Jack. The room is filled with the usual pungent cigar smoke. Thanks to that, the old man's B.O., and a waste basket filled with rancid food, the stench is sickening. Sammy wasn't the cleanest fucker when I first came to Funland, but now that he's a junkie he's gotten way worse. Thankfully, he doesn't have one of his skanks in here sucking him off. Bella was leaving when we arrived, and I wonder how she can stand sucking his nasty, funky dick. But then she's a meth-head too, and I've come to learn that meth-heads can put up with just about anything other than running out of meth.

The three of us look back and forth, trading knowing looks, but none of us comments.

"You guys probably wonder why I called you over," Sammy says, chewing black stuff out of his fingernails. It's interesting to watch him struggle to do this with a fat cigar sitting in the corner of his mouth.

"What's up?" Cracker Jack asks.

I'm not talking because I'm trying to keep my mouth shut so I won't breathe in more of the stench than I have to.

"I think we got a problem," Sammy says.

"What's that?" Cutter asks.

Sammy looks us over with a grim expression. "You guys remember the Bill White job, right? The one in Jeff City."

Of course we remember. How could we forget? It was the job of a lifetime for guys like us. It was thanks to that job that we're able to have new homes and cars.

"Sure," Cracker Jack says. "We remember."

"You guys heard Bill White is running for President, right?"

We have.

"I'm worried that sonofabitch might be on to us."

"Why you think that?" I ask.

"You remember that pig Grissom, right? The one who got us into this?" Sammy has become animated, causing his cigar to fall out of his mouth onto his lap. He does a half-sit, half-stand thing, knocking the lit cigar off his pants and onto the floor between the table and the recliner I'm in. He looks up at me. "Would you get that?"

I pick up the cigar. I hold it up, unsure what he wants me to do with it. He reaches his hand out. He's still short by a foot, so I have to stretch to hand it to him.

He sticks it back in his mouth.

"Okay," he says. "Where was I?"

"Grissom," I say.

"Right," he says. "So, Grissom's partner called me this morning and said both Grissom and his dumb whore sister were killed."

We all sit forward.

"What do you mean?" Cutter asks.

"What the hell do you think I mean?"

"How did it happen?" I ask.

"Were they killed together?" Cracker Jack asks.

"No, separately," Sammy says. "He said Grissom's sister got run off the road by another car a couple days ago. Hit a tree, broke her neck, and she was gone."

"Who did it?" I ask.

Sammy holds his palms up. "They don't know. Hit and run."

"Maybe it wasn't related," Cracker Jack says.

"Maybe," Sammy says. "But Marshall says Grissom was real upset. Then the next night—*last night*—someone broke into Grissom's house and shotgunned him and his family."

"Holy fuck," I say.

Sammy is biting his lip. He's trembling, but it's not that he's scared so much as it is that he's junked out of his mind. "Marshall says no one has come to see him yet, but he's scared. He thinks Bill White is gonna have him killed."

"Maybe those things aren't related," I suggest.

Sammy looks at me with dead eyes. "Bullshit. They've gotta be related. Either way, we're not taking a chance. Marshall's hiding, waiting to see what turns up. I'm supposed to call him on a burner if I hear anything. He's staying at a friend's cabin on the lake."

He stops talking and puffs on his cigar. Then he says, "We're gonna kill Marshall before Bill White gets to him. Maybe they don't know about us. They shotgunned Grissom in bed, so it don't sound like they questioned him. I don't understand it, but that's what Marshall said. We don't need Bill White sending his goons over here. The fucking guy's about to be President, so he could make things rough for us. If his goons don't kill us, he could pull government strings. We don't need that. We gotta kill Marshall."

"Let me do it," Cutter says. He's got that bloodthirsty look in his eyes, like he's hungry to kill.

"I don't care who does it," Sammy says. "But it's gotta be today. We can't leave loose ends that'll bring those fuckers here."

FIFTY-FOUR

CRACKER JACK ENDS up taking the job because he doesn't want to lose his spot as Sammy's hitter now that Gummy the albino is on the payroll. None of us have met Gummy and he never works in the Branson area, but Cracker Jack is worried.

Cracker Jack wanted me to ride to the cabin with him. Cutter decided not to come. Things between he and Kammie have been rocky lately, so he used their fighting as an excuse, saying he really needed to stay home and work things out. Cracker Jack and I know Cutter, and we both know better. He's just upset about Cracker Jack killing the cop instead of him.

I'm driving a stolen Subaru. As we head to the cabin, we talk about Sammy's paranoia. Cracker Jack has been overly loyal to Sammy, but he speaks honestly this time. In fact, he's the one who brings it up.

"What do you think about Sammy?" he asks.

I hesitate. "What do you mean?"

"You know what I mean."

"I think maybe he's doing too much crank."

Cracker Jack nods. "It's fuckin' with his head."

"It's been bad for a minute."

"It's worse now."

"You think Bill White knows about us?" I ask.

"Hell if I know." He sits in silence for a moment. "I don't mind doing the work, but lately it seems like Sammy's a little quick to pull the trigger."

"You mean quick to make *us* pull the trigger."

Cracker Jack makes a pained expression.

"You ever think about getting outta this life?" I ask.

"Not once." He looks at me. "You?"

I realize immediately I've potentially screwed myself. If Cracker Jack thinks I wanna leave Funland, he could tell Sammy, which would cause problems I don't need.

"Of course not. What am I gonna do, get a job at McDonalds?"

I laugh, but Cracker Jack doesn't. I can feel him staring at me. I don't know what he's thinking, but my paranoia tells me he's sizing me up, trying to determine whether I'm still loyal.

FIFTY-FIVE

Once we locate the gravel road snaking into the woods, I pull off onto it, driving back into the trees. Thankfully, the cabin is the only house on the road. I stop at a place in the road that's obscured from both the highway and the cabin.

"Wait here and keep watch," Cracker Jack says, raising his Glock. "I'll be back quicker than you can say dead cop."

"Dead cop."

Cracker Jack smiles. "Okay, funnyman." He gets out and disappears into the woods so he can approach the cabin from the side.

I sit for a few minutes, keeping watch until my phone rings. I pick it up to see who it is. It's Kammie. I answer. "What do you need?"

"You know what I need."

I sigh. "Kammie."

"Just listen, okay?"

"You've got one minute."

"I know you like me," she says.

"We've had this conversation."

"You get pissed at me, but you never block my number."

There's a part of me that enjoys the attention. And I get satisfaction from not giving in to her. She's right. For once in her life, Kammie's right. I need to block her number.

"It's because you want me too," she says.

"I don't."

"Listen Billy, I'm gonna tell you how it is."

"Oh yeah?" I say. "How is it?"

"I'm sure Cutter's told you, but we've been fighting lately."

"He doesn't have to tell me. I live next door. I can hear you both screaming at the top of your lungs."

"He thinks I'm cheating on him," she says.

"I'm sure you are."

"He's paranoid."

There's a lot of that going around.

"Here's the deal," she says, "you can either fuck me, and not just fuck me but fuck me *good*, or..."

"Or what?"

"I'll tell him we're fucking anyway."

"We're not though."

"I'll still tell him."

I sit for a moment, trying to process her ultimatum.

"You're a crazy bitch," I say.

"But you like it."

Cracker Jack emerges from the woods.

"I would never do that to Grace or Cutter," I say. "Then there's the other thing."

"What's that?"

"That you're a cunt." I click off only seconds before Cracker Jack opens the door. He climbs inside.

"How'd it go?" I ask.

"Shitty, that's how."

I look at him, trying to read his expression. He has a pained look on his face. "The cop was already dead when I got there."

"Dead?"

He nods solemnly. "Dead." He pauses for a beat. "Not just dead —dead without a head."

"They cut his head off?"

"No. They blew it all over the walls."

FIFTY-SIX

I DROPPED Cracker Jack off at Funland. I wasn't there when he delivered the news to Sammy, but I'm certain it didn't go well. Sammy was already paranoid, and this won't help. Christ. I should probably avoid him for a couple of days, which is what I do most of the time anyway. I could tolerate him when he was just an asshole, but him being a paranoid whacked-out asshole is a different story. When Sammy gets paranoid, people die. That means Cutter and me have to do it. Then there's always the concern Sammy might turn on me one day.

Things at home aren't great. Grace is still pissed about me working at Funland.

She and I are standing in the kitchen. She's nursing Gil, and I'm trying to calm her.

"I told you, just give me a year," I say. "That's all I need."

"I can't live like this for another year!"

I stare at her, trying to figure out how to end this discussion. "It hasn't been so bad. What's so bad about it? Nothing bad has happened to us. We've got nice things—nice vehicles, nice clothes, a new house. And everyone here treats us like family. What's one more year?"

"A hell of a lot," she says. "And things aren't perfect. *Family?* Some family! These are garbage people, Billy! Everything here is bad. Everything."

"What's so bad?" I say. "Tell me one bad thing!"

"I'll give you a hundred!"

"Okay, give me a hundred!"

She breaks down into tears. "Cops come to our house and go through our stuff every month. And for what? So we can give them an envelope filled with cash!"

I'm stunned. "You know about that?"

She glares at me through tears. "I'm not stupid, Billy. And then there's the FBI... That Winner guy has stopped me twice now."

"Warner," I correct.

She stares at me with dagger eyes. "That's not the point."

"What is it the point?"

She looks at me and relaxes a little, like she's so tired she no longer has the energy for this. "I don't want you to go to prison."

I put my hand on her shoulder and lean my head towards hers. We both look down at Gil. "I'm not going to jail," I say. "Nobody goes to prison."

She looks up at me angrily. "What the hell does that mean? A lot of people go to prison."

"Dummies," I assure her. "*Dummies* go to prison."

"My brother went to prison!"

"See?"

"I'm sorry," she says, "but your friends are not all that smart either. Cutter and Cracker Jack, they're..." She looks at me and decides not to finish. Instead she says, "Sammy is really stupid. Incredibly stupid. And, and... and he's *gross!*"

"I love you, Gracie Girl," I say. "You know that, don't you? Do you think I would ever do anything to hurt either of you?"

She looks at me with sad green eyes. "I don't think you'd hurt us on purpose. But there are some things you can't control."

"One year," I say. "Please, baby, give me a year. I just need time to figure this out."

"What do you need to figure out?"

"I need an exit strategy. I want—" I'm cut short by the roar of a car revving up outside. Before it even registers what the sound is, there's the sound of the vehicle peeling out.

Grace peers out through the blinds. "Kammie," she says.

I give Grace a half-hearted smile. "Of course."

My phone buzzes, informing me I've got a text. I pull the phone out of my pocket and look to see who it is. It's Cutter. His message reads: WE NEED 2 TALK, U RAT FUKK.

Jesus. Kammie's spilled the beans about our nonexistent affair.

I sigh. Grace asks who it is. I try my best to act normal. "It's Cutter. He wants to talk about Kammie."

"I'm sure he does," Grace says, exhaling hard. "I'm tired of listening to them argue. They're like children. I'm sure one of them cheated again."

"That's a given."

I text Cutter back: LET ME FINISH UP HERE AND I'LL BE OVER IN 10 MINUTES.

Cutter responds within seconds: FUKK U, COKKSUCKER.

FIFTY-SEVEN

I SPEND the next few minutes making peace with Grace and hoping Cutter doesn't burst in screaming that I fucked Kammie. That definitely would not help matters. Then Grace and Cutter would get into it, and everyone would hate everyone else. And if Cutter got angry and disrespected Grace... I don't even wanna think about it. Thankfully, none of this happens.

Grace and I agree to put the conversation on hold until later. She believes I'm gonna be a nice friend, comforting Cutter, but the truth is I'm terrified he's gonna shoot me or worse.

Once everything is smoothed over and Grace and Gil are settled in on the couch, I step out of the double-wide into the sunlight. I see Cracker Jack's F-10 sitting in front of Cutter's place. I'm relieved to see it, because if Cracker Jack is there, Cutter will be less likely to do something stupid. But I'm still smart enough to be nervous.

I walk up the steps and onto the porch. The front door is closed. Before I can knock, I hear the roar of a gunshot inside. I step aside so I can figure out what's happening and keep from being shot. I hear a second gunshot. I grab the Walther from my waistline and raise it just before the door opens. I see Cracker Jack's head emerge. He looks over at me and his eyes get big. I know immediately that he killed Cutter. My anger flares and I rush him, smashing him back against the door frame. He howls in pain and I'm pushed up against him when I pull the trigger, blasting him in the gut. He screams in agony, pushing me off. He staggers back, reaching for his gun. I shoot him center mass.

His empty hand drops away from his waist and he stumbles sideways, falling down the steps and crashing hard to the pavement. I walk to the top of the steps, standing over him, and I fire another round into his head. Then I go inside, finding Cutter dead on the floor, like I knew I would. I stare at him for a long moment before I realize I'm crying. And it's not just my eyes welling up; I'm crying, *hard*.

So, this is how it ends. Sammy's paranoid ass saw Cutter and me as loose ends, and he sent Cracker Jack to tie them. Goddammit, Cracker Jack, I think. I looked at you like a father figure. I loved you, man. What the hell. Did you think that Sammy would let you live? That he would overlook the fact that you were with us on the Bill White job? Cracker Jack was so blinded by his loyalty for Sammy —*unearned loyalty*—that he couldn't see the truth.

What about the other guys who were with us in Jeff City? Are they dead too? But there's no time to worry about them. I've gotta tie up my own loose ends and get the fuck outta Dodge.

FIFTY-EIGHT

WHEN I WALK BACK to the double-wide, Grace is standing in the doorway, holding Gil. "Did I hear gunshots?"

"Well," I say, "I've got good news and I've got bad news."

FIFTY-NINE

I STROLL into Funland like it's just another day. I don't wanna invite any unwanted attention, so I keep my head down and my mouth shut. But as I'm making my way through the fairway, Linda spots me. *"Hey Billy!"* I stop to humor her, and she approaches me. She looks distraught. "Didja hear about Cunny Jaymes?"

"No," I say. "What about him?"

"He killed hisself."

Well, fuck. That answers my question about whether or not Sammy is killing everyone involved with the Bill White heist.

"They say it was autoerotic asphyxiation. But I don't believe it." She leans in towards me. "Cunny's dick didn't even work. He told me his dick hadn't gotten hard since Bill Clinton was in office."

I wonder if this is true or just a story Cunny told Linda so he wouldn't hurt her feelings. After all, Linda has a dog face. Sure, I've fucked her a bunch of times, but I'm a sick fuck.

"Thanks for telling me," I say. "But I gotta go."

"Okay, sure. Maybe we can talk later."

"Sure," I say, already walking away. I've got nothing against

Linda, but right now the only thing on my mind is finding that miserable fuck Sammy and killing him.

I make my way through the park, keeping my eyes peeled for unexpected bullshit, but there is none.

I'm in the trailer area now, walking between trailers. I pass a couple carnies, but they pay me no mind.

When I arrive at Sammy's trailer, I look around, but see no one. I pull out the Walther and wrap my other hand around the doorknob. It turns easily and I swing the door open, pushing the pistol inside. Sammy is leaned back at the table with his eyes shut, smoking his cigar, getting head from Bella, who's naked as a jaybird. Her bare feet stick out from under the table and their soles are dog shit brown. I step inside, but neither of them knows I'm here. I pull the door shut, and they both startle. Bella bumps her head on the bottom of the table. They both reposition themselves to look at me.

Sammy's eyes get big. "Billy." That's all he manages, and the look of shock on his face tells the tale.

I point the Walther at Bella and wave it towards the door. "Get out."

She crawls out from beneath the table awkwardly. I haven't seen her naked in more than a year. She's got a few new ink pieces that look like jailhouse tats, and her once smooth-as-a-baby cunt looks like Don King.

"Can I get my clothes?" she asks.

I point the pistol at her. "Get out or die. Your choice."

Bella is visibly shaken. She presses her chin against her chest and heads for the door, sliding past me. I keep the Walther trained on Sammy. Once Bella is gone, I say, "Any last words?"

He chuckles, surprising me. "Bonesaw Billy," he says. "Bonesaw fuckin' Billy. I always figured it would come to this."

"What do you mean?"

"You didn't remember me, but I remembered you."

What the hell is he talking about?

His smile widens. "We met once. Back in Shreveport."

I have no idea what he's talking about.

"You were just a kid," he says. "But I was there. In the trailer."

"What trailer?"

"*Your* trailer. With your mama."

I still don't understand. I tilt my head, trying to comprehend. Then he says, "I was the one who cut that bitch's throat."

I'm speechless. I forget I've got the gun on him. Suddenly I'm transported back in time and I'm eight again, walking in to find my mom lying dead in a bloody mess in the front room of our trailer.

"I don't believe you," I say.

But I do.

There's a gleam in his eye. "I almost cut her fuckin' head off. When I came outta the trailer, I waved at you. And you waved back." He chuckles. "You remember. You don't wanna, but you do."

I concentrate now and it comes back to me. I see his fat ass in my mind's eye, grinning and waving.

"You know," he says, "I almost killed you, too."

He giggles, and his giggling snaps me back into the moment. I move forward and jam the pistol into his face. As he grimaces and pulls back, I pick up the ink pen lying on the table.

"Look at me," I say. His eyes are clenched as tightly shut as he can manage. "*Look at me!*" This does the trick and his eyes open. When they do, I jab that ink pen into his eye. Then I pull it back and jab it in, pull it out, jab it in, pull it out, over and over. Sammy's body convulses some, but by the twentieth or thirtieth jab of the pen, it's stopped. My final jab buries the pen in his eye, lodging itself deep in soft brain tissue.

SIXTY

As I TURN TO LEAVE, the door swings open and Bella is standing there naked, pointing a .45 at me. I raise the Walther, but she fires first, hitting me in the shoulder. The impact knocks me back, causing my muscles to spasm, making me squeeze off a round involuntarily. The Walther roars, sounding like an M-80 exploding in a coffee can, and Bella's teeth implode. I wobble a little, and it occurs to me that the bullet isn't the worst thing that's been in Bella's mouth today.

The other carnies will be arriving any minute to investigate the gun shots. I shove the Walther down into my jeans so hard it pokes my dick. I pull my shirt down over it and stalk back through the trailers. Someone a couple trailers down is grilling burgers, and the smell makes my empty stomach rumble. I've almost cleared the trailer area when I see Funland's resident strongman, Ernie Brinkman poke his fat head out from his trailer. He looks at me with the dumbest of dumb expressions. "You hear somethin'?"

I shrug, still walking. "Nah, not a thing."

Ernie looks off in the direction of Sammy's trailer, and I dip out of sight.

Somehow, I make it back to the parking lot without being

stopped. When I reach Grace and Gil waiting in Cracker Jack's pickup, I say, "Time to go."

Grace looks at me with those big, pretty green eyes. "Where we gonna go?"

I have no idea.

SIXTY-ONE

I DECIDED to head for Mexico. Grace suggested I call that FBI guy, Warner, but I told her I couldn't now that there's blood on my hands that can't be hidden. Besides, there's no one left for me to rat out; everyone's dead.

We got on US Highway 65 North and drove up to Springfield, where we pulled the pickup into a Walmart parking lot. I pointed at a black 1990-something Grand Cherokee on the outer edge of the lot. "How about that?" I asked. "That should be big enough for the three of us. Then we'll go down the road and boost another." Grace agreed. She looked at me and asked, "What do we do if the owner comes out before you're done?" I smiled and told her that the cars parked on the outer edge of the lot generally belonged to employees. "How'd you know that?" she asked. I winked at her and informed her that I was once a Walmart employee for a whole six hours. Then I got out and walked over to the Grand Cherokee. I got lucky and found it unlocked. I was rusty, but I managed to hotwire it in five or six minutes. Soon we were back on the road.

We reached Tulsa around midnight. We drove up and down backstreets, searching for a suitable vehicle to replace the Grand

Cherokee. Grace really liked the SUV and asked me to find another. I told her I would if I could. The problem was, all the newer vehicles had computer systems and fancy keys that made it difficult to steal them. Since I was looking for an older vehicle, that limited my options. It took a half hour, but I finally found a green Chevy van parked on a dark street. Grace didn't love the van, but she settled for it. This one was locked, but I used a screwdriver to bust the lock. Then I climbed in and went to work. I had a hell of a time getting it thing started. Eventually I did, though, and we climbed in with the baby seat and the two suitcases and took off. We were hungry and out of gas, so we pulled up to the pumps at a 7-11. I got out and pulled out my wallet but then realized I couldn't use my debit card. At least not if I didn't want to be found immediately.

So here we are. I climb back into the van and Grace asks, "What's wrong?" I say, "We can't use our cards, and we don't have any cash." I pull the van around to the side of the 7-11. I park the van and Grace looks at me. "Do you think they have the capability to track us?"

"Yes," I say. "Sammy had the capability, and the authorities *definitely* have the capability."

She blinks. *"The authorities?* You think the cops are after us?"

"They will be. There's a bloodbath at Cutter's place, and Sammy and Bella were both shot to shit at Funland."

"You shot Bella?"

I just nod. "Since we've disappeared, it's gonna be pretty obvious we're connected somehow."

She wrinkles her face and stares out the window. "Maybe they'll think we're dead."

"Either way, they're gonna be looking."

She sinks down into her seat. She's still holding our sleeping son. "What now?" she asks.

I give her my best million-dollar smile. "Have I ever let you down, Gracie Girl?" She gives me a weary look and I feel guilty. "You strap Gil into his car seat in back while I go in. I'm gonna take care of this. But strap him in quickly."

"What are you gonna do?"

I grin. "You know what I do, baby."

I get out and take about ten steps towards the store. Then a thought occurs to me, and I walk back to Grace. "You got a baby blanket?"

"What do you need it for?"

"Don't worry about it," I say. "Do you have one?"

She reaches in and pulls a baby-blue blanket from the baby bag. She hands it to me. I reach into my pocket and pull out my pocketknife. Then I cut eye holes in the blanket. They look awful and they're too small, so I tug the knife, making the holes bigger. They look worse than shitty, but they'll do the trick. I pull the shirt over my head, using it as a makeshift mask. I try to line up the eye holes, but they're crooked no matter how I turn the blanket.

"Fuck," I mutter as I head towards the front of the store. I slide the Walther out from my waistline.

SIXTY-TWO

THERE ARE CUSTOMERS IN 7-11. No matter what time you go into a 7-11, there are always people fucking around buying Slurpees and whatnot. There are three cars parked out front—all miraculously empty —and no vehicles at the pump. But this could change in an instant, so time is of the essence. I stride towards the entrance, looking inside to see where everyone is. I see a woman staring into the doughnut case and a fat redneck in a muscle shirt perusing the pops in front of the cooler. I see the clerk, a young Indian guy with glasses, standing behind the counter looking down. As I take my last steps towards the door, I look for the driver of the third car and conclude he's probably in the bathroom. If I do this thing right, I'll be gone before his turd hits the water.

I pull the door open and step inside. When I do, the clerk looks up and sees my shitty blue mask and my Walther out in front. I point it at him. Now Doughnut Bitch turns and looks at me, dropping her coffee and screaming. I point the Walther at the clerk and look across the store at Pop Guy so I can watch him.

"Gimme all the money in your drawer, you Indian fuck!" I scream.

The clerk stares at me like a deer caught in headlights.

I reposition the pistol. *"Do it, goddammit!"*

"I'm Pakistani."

I rush towards him with my pistol in his face. *"You're about to be dead, you cocksucker! Now empty that register!"*

He goes to the register. I look at the two customers, swiveling my gun in a sweep to cover them. *"You!"* I scream. *"Both of you! Get down on the goddamn floor!"*

Doughnut Cunt and Pop Fuck lower themselves to the floor, but the clerk, who now has the register open, asks, "Do you want me to get on the floor, too?"

"Jesus H Christ!" I scream in a suddenly hoarse voice. *"Gimme all the money! Give it to me now!"*

The clerk is shaking. As he reaches into the register drawer, I feel my blanket-mask sliding, so I reposition it so the eyes line up. When the clerk turns towards me, I've got the Walther aimed at him. He holds out the money and lays it on the counter.

"Could you at least give me a sack?" I ask. The guy shrugs and reaches down for one. He grabs a sack and lifts it, pushing the money into it. The moment the last dollar is in the sack, I start backing towards the door. I make a point to aim the Walther at the clerk, so he knows I'm talking to him. *"You get on the fucking floor too, fucko!"* He disappears behind the counter. My back is against the door. I turn to leave. I push the door halfway open when a gunshot rings out and a bullet strikes the candy rack on my left. I look and see a cowboy with a pistol standing back by the bathroom.

Instead of shooting it out like the Wild Bunch, I sprint past the front of the store towards the side where the van is parked. Another bullet shatters the front window of the 7-11. *"Holy fuck!"* I scream as I scramble for safety.

When I get to the van, I run around it and climb into the driver's seat. I drop the van into reverse and stomp the gas. Grace starts screaming hysterically. The van rockets back almost all the way to the street. There's another gunshot, and I hear it hit the passenger side mirror.

"Hold on!" I say. *"I'll get us outta here!"*

I stop and drop the thing into drive. There's another gunshot, which sounds like it hits the front headlight. I spin the van out and stomp the gas again. The van lurches forward and shoots out into the street, giving us a jolt. Baby Gil is crying now. I take a gulp of air, trying to catch my breath.

I turn and look at Grace. "I told you I'd get us out of this!"

As the last word leaves my mouth, I realize Grace has been shot in the chest. We're zipping down the street and I'm staring at her with tears in my eyes. The baby is still screaming.

"Are you alright, baby?" I ask. *"Grace? Grace?"*

But she doesn't answer.

SIXTY-THREE

THERE ARE tears in my eyes as I alternate, looking at the road, then Grace, the road, then Grace. *"Grace,"* I say. *"Please... Grace."* As I drive, it occurs to me. The "please" gives me the thought. I stare at the road ahead, gripping the steering wheel as tightly as I can. Baby Gil is howling.

"Please," I say. "God, if you're there, I need your help." I look over at Grace, who's still motionless. "Please God, please. I never asked you for shit. Never. *Ever.* I didn't ask you for help even when that fucker killed my mom. Not even when Uncle Boyd... did... Well, you know what he did... I never asked you for nothin', but I'm asking you now, and I think you owe me one on account of all the awful shit I've gone through and the fact I never asked before. Just this once, God. I'm asking you to save my Gracie Girl. Please save her. She's better than me, God. She's not like me. She's too good for this shit. *Please...*" I break down, and I'm sobbing hard. Gil is screaming his lungs out. "Please dear God, please, for Gil, please save her... Please..."

I look over at Grace and she's motionless. I look back at the road and a second crazy idea occurs to me. This one will be hard. I know it won't work, but I have to try. Even if it's bullshit, I have to, for Grace.

"God, if you save my Gracie Girl, I'll walk away from her forever," I say. "If you bring her back so she can take care of our son, I'll walk away from them both. I swear on everything, I'll leave, and I'll never see either one of them again." I pause and then add, "If I ever do, you can kill us all. Please, God. I'm asking this one and only favor and I'll never ask you for anything ever again."

I'm crying hard when I look over at Grace. She's still motionless. Still dead, just like I knew she would be. I take a deep breath and stare at the road ahead. I knew it. There's no God. I always suspected that was the case, but now I know.

And then I hear Grace's voice. "Billy," she says quietly, almost a whisper. I look over and her eyes are open. "I think I've been hit."

SIXTY-FOUR

"You've been hit, but you're gonna be okay," I say.

I drive to another gas station. I pull up to the pump. "You stay here," I tell her. "I'll be right back." I climb out, grabbing the 7-11 sack with the cash in it. I count the money for the first time. There's a grand total of $63. I almost lost Grace for a measly sixty-three bucks. And I remember my promise to God. The God I don't believe in.

I walk into the store. There are a couple of people inside. There's a young black woman standing in front of the counter. I wait for her to finish her business, then I step up and pay the old cashier for five bucks worth of gas. I ask him if he's familiar with the area. He says he is, so I ask him for directions. He gives them to me, I thank him, and I go back outside and pump the gas.

I climb inside the van. Grace whispers, "Do you think I'll be okay?"

I look into her beautiful green eyes. "Yes, baby."

It only takes me five minutes to find Utica street. I hook a right and drive until I get to Ascension St. John Medical. I pull into the parking lot. I make sure to park among a cluster of cars, way out away from the building. Baby Gil has apparently worn himself out and has fallen asleep.

"Where are we?" Grace asks.

"This is a hospital."

"What are we doing here?"

"I'm gonna get us a new car."

She nods. I look at her and whisper, "I love you, Gracie Girl. I've loved you since the first time I saw you."

She looks at me through tired, slitted eyes. "You're sweet, Billy."

I kiss my palm and touch it to her forehead.

"I'll be right back," I say. I look back at our sleeping son. "Take care of Gil."

Grace nods and closes her eyes. I get out and walk a couple of cars down, crying as I do. The lot is brightly lit, but there's no one out here. Just cars. I find an old silver Ford minivan. This'll do. As I approach the driver's side door, I wonder if I'm doing the right thing. When I pull the door handle, I find it unlocked. Maybe this is a sign. When I get in, I find the keys dangling from the ignition. I look out at the night sky, thinking God is a prick. In this moment, I remember the night Grace pointed out the Big Dipper. The night Cutter proposed to Kammie. It seems like a long time ago, but the memory warms my heart.

As I start the van, tears cascade down my face. I back out, taking one last look at the parked green van. Grace is asleep and doesn't see me.

"Goodbye, Gracie Girl," I say, and I drive away.

SIXTY-FIVE

YEAR EIGHT

GETTING a fake passport wasn't easy. It took a couple of weeks to find a guy and get it done. I had to hide out the entire time. I had to hide out and scrape together the money. I was forced to sell my beloved Walther PPK for a fraction of what it's worth. But it had bodies on it, so it wasn't like I could haggle. I broke into a couple of houses to get the rest. When I finally got a passport and caught a ride across the border, I was as scared as a Jew at a skinhead rally. But I got through.

Once I was in Mexico, I found myself with a brand-new set of problems. I had exactly $29—three in change—and no transportation. Not even a bike.

I once read a book about a Mexican city called El Rey where criminals could go for sanctuary, but it turned out El Rey was made up. Since I was broke, I wound up staying in Juarez, where I got a job sweeping and cleaning dishes in a bar called La Rata Sucia. The job pays shit, but the owner, a man named Gabriel, lets me stay in a room upstairs.

This is my life now. I work and squirrel away what money I can, but there's an emptiness inside that I cannot fill. I wonder every day what Grace and Gil are doing. For a while I worried Grace might have died waiting for me in that parking lot. My initial belief was that God would protect her since he had given her a second chance, but after a while I started to worry that maybe none of that had been real. Maybe Grace had never really been dead. But deep down, I know that's not the truth. After worrying for a few months, I finally borrowed Gabriel's cell phone and looked up Grace on social media. When I did, I saw that she had survived. I have no idea what she told the cops, but judging from the photos, she's living with her folks. There are photos of Gil, too, and he looks healthy and strong.

I miss them every day. I wonder what Grace believes happened. Does she think I was killed? Or does she think I just ran away, leaving her to die? But then, that's pretty much what happened, isn't it? No, I tell myself; I made a deal with God and I'm holding up my end. For once in my life, Billy Hanson is doing the right thing. Sometimes I consider going back, but I know I can't. I made a deal with God that he could take their lives if I do, and I have no reason to believe he wouldn't. I'm not a religious man, but I know what happened; I offered a deal to God and he accepted. Sometimes I entertain the thought that I misread those events and could go back, but I push those thoughts aside. I would never, ever endanger Grace and Gil. And let's be frank, even without the God bargain, my presence in their lives puts them in danger. So now I've not only vowed to God that I'll never go back, but I've also vowed it to myself.

I finally had to force myself to stop borrowing Gabriel's phone to check in on Grace. Looking her up accomplishes nothing. It only hurts me, teasing me with images of the life I could have had. After I borrowed the phone a couple more times, I finally resolved that I would chop off one of my fingers if I ever looked her up again. I will hold myself to this, just as I am holding myself to the vow I made to walk away.

I often wonder what's happening back home. I know a little. I know that our old pal Bill White is now President of the United States, which cracks me up. Can you believe that? We pulled one over on the most powerful man in the world! I also know that the Cardinals need help in the bullpen. I know there was a riot in New York City a few months back, but I have no idea what it was about.

Sometimes I wonder who's running Reverend Sammy's empire now. But then I also wonder if there even is an empire now. For all I know, Funland is as dead as its owner.

Sammy is dead, but I'm alive, even if it's in name only. The reality is that I'm as dead as my cohorts. I'm still breathing air, but I have no life. My life is a thousand miles away in Missouri.

SIXTY-SIX

THERE'S a big brick church down the street. I see it every day, and sometimes the priest, Padre Luis, has a few drinks in the bar. He's a nice man as far as I can tell. He jokes around and always looks happy. Whenever I see him looking so happy, I wish I was happy like him. Even now, after almost a year in Juarez, I speak very little Spanish. Most of the words I've learned are curse words, which don't do me much good. Because of this, I carry around a paperback English to Spanish dictionary. I read the words from the book, but I can tell by the Mexicans' faces what I'm saying is wrong. But it's usually close enough to the proper phrasing that they understand. It also helps that Gabriel speaks some English. It's not very good English, but it's better than my Spanish.

I've been considering a visit with Padre Luis for a while, but I keep putting it off. For some reason, the thought frightens me. But today I decide to face my fear and walk to the church. When I step inside, the sanctuary is empty. It feels like a tomb. I make my way past the pews, my footsteps clacking on the tile. I stop when I'm near the front, and I sit in the third row. I've never been to a Catholic church before, but the people I've seen on television are always lighting big candles with little candles. I don't know anything about this, so I don't mess with the candles. I look around, but don't see Padre Luis or anyone else for that matter. I sit quietly to wait. As I do, I ponder my life and the limited options I have, hoping perhaps answers might come more easily inside the house of the Lord.

I've been here for a half an hour now. I'm about to leave when I see Padre Luis walking along the wall across the sanctuary. He's heading down to the front. He doesn't see me. I stand and make my way through the pews. Padre Luis is sitting in the front row with his hands folded on his lap. I approach him from behind, startling him. He studies my face and smiles with recognition. I walk around to stand before him. I motion towards the seat to inquire if it's okay to sit. He nods, and his smile widens.

I sit down beside him. I smile and hold up my English to Spanish dictionary. He looks at it and grins. "I speak American."

"Oh, okay."

"I never have seen you before here." His English is pretty crappy, but again better than my Spanish.

"No," I say. "This is my first time."

He stares at me, waiting for me to continue.

"I have a question," I say. I point towards the ceiling. "About him... *God.*"

Padre Luis nods and grins. "Yes, yes, God. What is question you have?"

I speak slowly as if I were speaking to a slow child. "I made a deal with God. A *deal*. Do you understand deal?"

He nods, still smiling.

"I am trying to keep my agreement."

His brow furrows and his face twists with confusion. *"Keep?"*

"*Honor*," I say. "*Honor* the agreement."

He lights up with understanding.

"My question," I say, "is what will God do if I break our agreement?"

199

Padre Luis doesn't understand, so I explain it more clearly. He stares at me. "You *must* honor agreement."

"Will God be angry if I don't honor my agreement?"

Padre Luis nods. "Yes. Yes. God will be angry. Very important to honor."

I sit for a moment and consider this. I'm not convinced the priest even understands what I'm asking. But even if he doesn't understand, I believe he's right—God wants me to honor our agreement.

"Thank you," I say. When I stand to leave, Padre Luis reaches out to shake my hand. When I grab his hand and shake it, I see him staring at the nub where my pinky finger used to be.

SIXTY-SEVEN

IT'S STORMING outside when the idea arrives. It's not like I'd never considered it before, but it had never been more than a fleeting thought. But tonight is different. It's two a.m. and I'm four hours into a drinking session. The lights are out, and I'm sitting on the edge of my bed staring out the window, watching the lightning flash. Each time the lightning flashes, it lights up the room. It's hotter than the ninth circle of hell now. I stripped off my shirt an hour ago, but my body is slick with sweat.

The lightning flashes and in that instant, as if the lightning bolt struck my brain, the idea pops into my head like a statement followed by an exclamation point. Maybe it's just the fog of intoxication, but I don't question it. I just lean down and reach under my bed, fishing for the shoe box. My hand doesn't find it, so I have to get down on my knees to retrieve it. I slide the box out and pull it to my body, returning to my place on the edge of the bed. The box is in my lap. I take the lid off. It's dark in the room—dark until the next lightning flash—so I can't see the contents of the box. But I know what's there.

I reach over to the nightstand. I grab the tequila and take another swig. Then I set the bottle down and return my attention to the box. I reach inside and wrap my fingers around the .45 Gabriel sold me. All I want is to be happy, and since I can't be happy, I want to be dead.

I grip the .45, hefting its weight in my hand. Then, with the other hand, I reach into the box and pick up the clip. I insert it into the pistol. It's been a good run, but I'm ready. I want off this ride. I stare out the window into the rainy darkness and raise the pistol, touching its barrel to my temple.

I squeeze the trigger.

SIXTY-EIGHT

CLICK!

The pistol jams. I try again, but the result is the same.

Well, fuck. I could try again, but the moment has subsided, and I've lost the desire. Maybe later.

SIXTY-NINE

The following morning, I open the door to my room. It's only about a third of the way open and I see the big burly guy with pinkish skin and an almost white mohawk standing at the bar staring at Gabriel, who's on the phone.

There's no question this man is the infamous albino hitman Gummy. The one out of Kansas City who was supposed to be hot shit. And there's no doubt why he's here. He's here to kill me.

I close the door and scan my room. There's no other door. My only option is to climb out onto the roof. As I bolt towards the window, I wonder who sent Gummy. Who's left at Funland now that all my friends are dead? Perhaps he's simply come to avenge his boss. I slide the window open and look down at the street, seeing no one. I climb out onto the slanted roof. I have to hurry, or Gummy will be inside my room, shooting at me from the window. I hurriedly make my way towards the back of the building in the hopes there will be a safe place to jump. I take three or four steps and then lose my footing and stumble. I turn towards the roof and my stomach and face smack hard against it, and I'm sliding down the roof towards the edge. I almost manage to pull myself back up, but then fall back and tumble, falling over the edge.

I land hard on the cobblestone street. Somehow, I manage to get my feet down, but I land at an angle. My feet hitting the ground first probably breaks the velocity of the fall, and I fall on my ass and sort of roll onto my back. I lay on the cobblestones for a moment, stunned and gasping for air. My entire body hurts. I'm dazed, but the adrenaline kicks in, and before I know it, I'm back on my feet, wobbling like a drunk. I turn towards the bar and realize I left the pistol up in my room.

Now I'm good and fucked. I look towards the corner at the front of the bar, and no one's coming. I turn to my right in search of something I can use as a weapon. Gabriel's beat up old red pickup is parked on the side of the road at the rear of the bar. Its windows are down. Maybe there's something inside; a crowbar maybe. I'm moving more slowly than usual, and I hobble to the truck as stiffly as the Frankenstein monster. As I round the truck to the driver's side, I look up at the window to my room, but there's no albino head sticking out of it. The door is unlocked, and I swing it open and look inside, finding nothing useful. I close the door and look in the bed of the truck, where there's an assortment of crap. There's a metal gas can, some pieces of cut wood, and... an ax. I lean over the side of the truck, my back hurting as I do, and grab the wooden handle of the ax.

Ax in hand, I turn and hobble towards the front of the bar. When I reach the corner, I round it with the ax up over my head, but no one is there. I slowly approach the entrance. I'm only a few steps away when Gabriel steps out, startling me. His eyes get big when he sees me. He's got a cigarette in one hand and a lighter in the other. He looks at the ax, nods, and raises a finger of the hand holding the cigarette to his lips, telling me to be quiet. Then he turns and goes inside.

I stand there, out of sight from inside the entrance, holding the ax cocked like a ball bat. And I wait. I'm not confident this is the right move, but I do it anyway. My whole life has been a series of fuck ups, so why should now be any different? After a couple of minutes, I hear Gabriel's voice just inside the door say, "I have no idea where he go." As he speaks, his voice is getting closer. I cock the ax back a little bit tighter, ready to strike.

I hear Gabriel's voice again, "Good luck! Maybe you find him!"

A moment later, an unsuspecting Gummy steps out. He turns towards me with a cigarette in his mouth and before he can even register what he's seeing, I'm swinging that ax as hard as I can, and my swing is as sure as Mickey Mantle's. Gummy's eyes start to go wide just as the business end of the ax connects with his face. The axe smacks him hard and, even though he tumbles back, the ax head is buried in his face enough that it almost tears from my hands.

I stand there for a long moment staring at the dead albino, wondering who sent him. I look at Gummy's still lit cigarette lying on the ground, and I squat to retrieve it, my back hurting as I do. I pick up the cigarette and stick it between my lips.

A moment later, Gabriel returns. He raises his cigarette to his mouth and lights it. Then he looks at me. "You pretty good with that, gringo. Next time *you* chop the fuckin' wood."

SEVENTY

YEAR NINE

ONE AFTERNOON I'm on a supply run at the market with Gabriel and his fifteen-year-old son, Arturo. There's an elderly man staring at me. He doesn't look away, even after I've met his gaze. I wonder why he's looking at me, so I approach him. "*Hola!*" His stare transforms into an unmistakable glare. He spits the words "*basura americano*" at me, turns, and walks away.

Arturo chuckles. I look at him. "What the hell did he say?"

Gabriel smiles big now. "*Basura americano,*" he says. "American trash."

SEVENTY-ONE

Iт's the middle of the night. I'm in my room, drinking in the dark. I'm sitting on my bed with my back flat against the wall. I've been downing whiskey for hours, and there's only about a fifth of the bottle left. I lay my head back against the wall and close my eyes, picturing my Gracie Girl in her wedding dress, looking at me with those big, gorgeous green eyes.

I'm lost in my own world, so I'm startled by the familiar voice. "Same old Billy," Cutter says. My eyes pop open, and I stare at him, nothing more than a silhouette sitting on the end of the bed in darkness.

I squint, trying to see him. I can't see his face, but I recognize his shape. "*Cutter?*" I ask. "*Is that you?*"

I know it can't be, but it is.

There's laughter in his voice when he asks, "Who the hell else would it be?" He says it like it should be obvious, like he's forgotten he's dead. I'm so happy he's here that I don't bring it up. I just stare at his silhouette, confused, happy, and drunk. There are tears in my eyes, and I'm glad it's dark so he can't see them.

"Did I ever tell you about the time Arlo Cahill asked me to bang his wife?" he asks. Of course he has. Like all of his sex stories, Cutter's told me this a dozen times. But I don't say anything, and he doesn't wait for me to answer.

"She was a good-lookin' broad, that one. But I didn't want old Arlo to watch me pound her." He chuckles. "That was his thing, you know? That was the whole deal; he was asking 'cause he wanted to watch. Can you believe that? Lowlife fuckin' degenerate."

I chuckle and say something in agreement, but nothing so substantial that Cutter feels the need to stop talking. "I said, 'Yeah, sure Arlo. I'd be glad to do that for ya!' So, I went over to his apartment and I drank wine with them and got good and drunk. We all did. The whole time I was flirting with the guy's wife, Britney. And I could tell she was into me."

No one can tell a story like Cutter, and I mean *no one*. This guy missed his calling. He shoulda been a comedian or a talk show host instead of a criminal.

"So, Britney's rubbin' my shaft, and I'm harder than Chinese arithmetic," Cutter says, really getting into it. "I'm pokin' outta my jeans and I can see in Britney's eyes that she wants it."

I already know what happens next, but I egg him on. "What did you do then?"

Cutter laughs. "I sent Arlo out to get the box of rubbers outta the glove compartment in my car. Then he went outside, and I locked the door and fucked her right there against it. He was outside knocking and banging, and I was inside, *also knocking and banging!* And let me tell you, that girl was into it! She was moaning like a banshee. Then, after we got done, I gave her a kiss on her forehead and walked out. When I did, the fuckin' guy was just sittin' in the hallway cryin' like a baby."

But that's not the payoff. I already know it, and I'm waiting in anticipation like a concertgoer waiting for the signature song.

"And you know what?" Cutter says. "Britney got pregnant! And they had the baby! It was a boy, and the fuckin' guy named it Arlo Jr.! The fuckers had *my baby!* Can you believe that?"

Of course I can't because it's a made-up story. I don't even think Arlo and Britney are real people, despite Cutter's tendency to drop their and a hundred other fantasy people's names into his stories. And I don't care. Right now, I'm just happy to see my friend.

His head turns towards me and I can tell he's looking at me, even though I can't see his face. "You know what?" he says. "That was pretty fucked up what Cracker Jack did to me."

"What?"

"The fuckin' guy killed me. Whaddaya think I'm talkin' about?"

"Cutter?" I ask. "How are you here?"

He laughs a loud, hearty laugh. "I'm *not* here, dummy. I'm fuckin' dead!"

SEVENTY-TWO

I REMEMBER the dream vividly the next morning, and it makes me sad. Sad because I miss my best friend. Sad because I'm all alone. In one way or another, everyone I ever loved is gone.

Now it's just me, living out each day like an endless sentence in hell.

SEVENTY-THREE

Iт's a Sunday morning and I'm sitting at the bar. The place is almost empty. There's some Mexican music playing over the speakers, but I don't know what the hell they're singing about, and to tell you the truth this shit all sounds the same to me. Gabriel is working the bar, and he's down at the other end, sitting on a stool reading a book. I'm smoking a cigarette and drowning my miseries in whiskey.

I look at the mirror on the wall in front of me and see the American the moment he walks in. I've never seen him before. He's coming towards me, and I know it's trouble. As he moves towards me from behind, Gabriel addresses him. "What you need, man?" The young, good-looking, sandy-blonde man answers, "Nothing, thank you." He sidles up beside me and puts his arm around me. I feel the pistol in his other hand poking into my ribs. He leans in and his breath is warm as he whispers, "Bill White sends his regards."

Bill White? This catches me off guard. Before I can respond, Gabriel racks the shotgun. Blondie hears it too, and we both turn to look at him.

"No, Gabriel," I say. "It's okay."

Gabriel looks confused. He stands there with the shotgun trained on Blondie. I hold up my hand, showing Gabriel my palm. "He's a friend."

Gabriel slowly lowers the shotgun. I can see he doesn't believe me, but he does what I ask.

I look into Blondie's eyes. "Let's go out to the alley. No one will bother us there."

He nods. I finish my drink and stand. I nod at Gabriel and walk outside with Blondie right behind. When we reach the door, he says, "Don't try any slick shit."

I laugh a tired laugh. "No worries. If I was gonna do that, I woulda let Gabriel blow you to pieces." I lead him around the building. Once we're in the alley, I turn and look at him. I hold my hands out to my side to show him I'm not a threat.

"Can you give Bill White a message?" I ask.

Blondie looks confused, but says, "Sure."

"Tell him thanks for the money. I had a lot of fun spending it."

Blondie grins.

"One more thing," I say. "Make it a clean shot."

Blondie nods and raises the Glock, pointing it in my face. He stares at me. "One thing first." I nod and he asks, "Why are you making this so easy?"

I sigh. "I'm tired. I'm just ready to go."

Blondie nods and his finger tenses on the trigger. I close my tear-filled eyes and smile, picturing my Gracie Girl and Baby Gil in my mind's eye.

THE END

Dear reader,

We hope you enjoyed reading *American Trash*. Please take a moment to leave a review, even if it's a short one. Your opinion is important to us.

Discover more books by Andy Rausch at https://www.nextchapter.pub/authors/andy-rausch

Want to know when one of our books is free or discounted? Join the newsletter at http://eepurl.com/bqqB3H

Best regards,

Andy Rausch and the Next Chapter Team

Lightning Source UK Ltd.
Milton Keynes UK
UKHW011845241120
374038UK00001B/98